Matilda Jerningham

Random rhymes

From January to December

Matilda Jerningham

Random rhymes
From January to December

ISBN/EAN: 9783337264895

Printed in Europe, USA, Canada, Australia, Japan

Cover: Foto ©Andreas Hilbeck / pixelio.de

More available books at **www.hansebooks.com**

RANDOM

RHYMES,

FROM

January to December.

BY

MRS. JERNINGHAM.

PRINTED BY SHERWOOD & Co.
N. W. Corner Baltimore and Gay Streets.

PREFACE.

THE solicitation of numerous friends has induced the publication of this volume. As the title implies, "RANDOM RHYMES" are the production of leisure hours of a "busy life," and as such, with their merits and imperfections, are submitted to the generous consideration of the reader.

> "He either fears his fate too much,
>   Or his deserts are small,
> Who dares not leave them to the touch,
>   And by it stand or fall."

MRS. JERNINGHAM.

BALTIMORE,
   November, 1873.

CONTENTS.

RANDOM RHYMES.

JANUARY.

January, with mantle warm,
Is battling with the gathering storm,
The earth is clothed with coat of mail,
Closely she folds her robe and veil;
The joy-bells at her birth were rung,
And happy voices carols sung,
To hail the first-born of the year,
Proclaiming her both *good* and *fair*.

The fleecy snow is falling fast,
Loud and shrill the wintry blast,
No birds are heard in leafy grove,
To chant her praise with songs of love,
No radiant flowers to bind her hair,
Snow-wreaths are glancing everywhere,
Over the mountain, in the vale,
Rings out Old Winter's piercing gale.

The hoar-frost glitters on the plain,
The river wears the ice-king's chain,
Yet the bright virgin, young and fair,
Proclaims the advent of the year :
Now, hour by hour, and day by day,
Earth brightens 'neath her onward way,
Less rugged looks the barren ground,
Less sad the wintry breezes sound.

Under the snow, the quickening earth
Shelters the young roots' tender birth ;
As yet the nymph folds robe and veil,
Her hidden beauty to conceal,
But as the sunlight gilds the scene,
Nature will show her emerald green,
And with its daily brightening ray,
Chase from the earth Old Winter's sway.

Oh ! month of myriad hopes and fears,
Beneath thy sway we dry our tears ;
As worthy labor wealth commands,
We will no longer fold our hands,
But build our " castles in the air,"
Bright as thy presence *Januare*,
And when at last we sound thy knell,
Joy-bells shall ring thy kind Farewell.

"HOPE ON, HOPE EVER."

Hope on, hope ever!
Every dark cloud
That hides the bright sun's golden beams,
   In time may show a silver lining,
Bright as life morning's radiant dreams.
   The wintry storm, though keen and angry,
Cleanses the earth from blight and rot,
   And, when the fresh bud bursts its bondage,
         Is soon forgot.

Hope on, hope ever!
Time is passing,—
Day succeeds day with rapid speed;
   Our brief life is the only season
To plant, to plow, to sow good seed.
   And as we sow, so shall the harvest
Bring the glad sheaves of golden grain,
   Or the dank weeds of woe and wailing,
         Life's heritage of joy or pain.

Hope on, hope ever!
In creation
Man hath no lasting place on earth;
   As hour by hour, the Present ever
Yields to the Future's mystic birth.
   The Past may hang its funeral flowers,
Closing the tomb with garlands fresh and gay;
   "Hope on, hope ever!" still shall be our motto
         To lead us to eternal day.

A WINTER SCENE.

The snowy crest of Winter
   Is glancing everywhere,
Trembling on the forest trees,
   That lately were so bare;
Glancing on the hill-tops,
   Cowering in the vale,
Drifting by the cottage door,
   Riding on the gale;
Dancing o'er the silver lake
   Encased with coat of mail,
Covering every object,
   With a light and graceful veil;
Mixing with the sullen sea,
   Melting as it falls,
Resting on the rugged steps
   Of ocean's frowning halls.

How charming is the landscape,
   When the storm hath sunk to rest,
And the mid-day sun looks coldly down,
   On nature's spotless vest:
From cottage eaves, and forest trees,
   The icicle depends,
Whilst magic tracery on the glass,
   A soft enchantment lends;

It seems as if a fairy hand
 Had built a crystal palace,
Set round with bright transparent spars,
 Shed from a silver chalice ;
Whilst struggling into life, the trees
 Shake off the melting snow,
And wandering o'er the glistening earth,
 The wintry breezes blow.

But when the silver moon appears,
 Queen of the silent night,
Surrounded by the starry host,
 That gladden earth with light,
When fitful shadows stalk around,
 Beneath her silvery beams,
'Tis then "old memories of the past,"
 Arise in pensive dreams ;
The well-beloved—the sacred dead,
 Our earliest friends appear,
And long forgotten voices seem
 To greet the listening ear ;
Our souls expand, our spirits soar
 To realms more pure and blest,—
"Where the wicked cease from troubling,"
 "And the weary are at rest."

"BE KIND TO EACH OTHER."

" Be kind to each other.
The night's coming on,
When friend and when brother
Alike shall be gone."—CHARLES SWAIN.

Well hath the poet sung,
  It is a thrilling chord,
How many bosoms have been wrung
  By a cold or careless word?
A look of pride or scorn
  Can chill the warm heart's glow,
And teach us here to mourn
  On our pilgrimage below.

The human heart still clings,
  Through sunshine, storm and shade,
As its hopes and joys it flings
  Round the shrine its own faith made:
A holy resting-place,
  So long as none can breathe
The baleful air of fell disgrace,
  Where its trembling tendrils wreathe.

But let suspicion's frown,
　Or doubt's tyrannic sway,
Upon its faith look down,
　And its freshness fades away ;
And the heart feels sad and scar,
　And wakes with shuddering chill,
As 'midst its flowers appear
　The hemlock roots of ill.

Oh ! let thy words be kind,
　Thy deeds above disguise,
And then thou'lt surely find
　Where this world's pleasure lies.
'Tis not in wealth or fame—
　Both, both will quickly fade,
As e'en the fairest name
　Will own some transient shade.

Watch well thy erring heart,
　Guard from each dangerous snare
That assails its weakest part,
　But thy friend and neighbor spare !
And if thou hast a foe,
　Teach him, by being kind,
The strongest link below
　Humanity can bind.

MUSINGS.

The Past!   How like a dream appear
   The records of the past!
How frail the stems too oft are proved
   Round which our hopes are cast;
Round which the tendrils of the heart
   In happier hours have twined,
When those we loved and trusted most
   Were faithful, good and kind!

The Past!   What visions at those words,
   Come thronging o'er the heart,
What memories of the griefs and joys,
   In which we've borne our part;
The joys our happy childhood knew,
   The happiness of home,
How like an angel's wings of light
   Such memories to us come!

Who hath not sighed, who hath not smiled
   Almost unconsciously;
Yet knew no gladness in the smile,
   No misery in the sigh?
A dream of youth had passed away,
   And left a void behind,
Whose scar would still remain to prove
   Some wound had there been joined.

Time is the power that only can
    Tear from our eyes the veil,
That false ones wear when their own hearts
    From us they would conceal ;
Time only proves the true heart's links
    Can twine when we have known,
That life hath thorns amidst the flowers
    We fondly deemed our own.

The Present ! all that we can claim,
    Would we redeem the Past,
An atom in our thread of life,
    Still fleeting as the last !
The breath we draw, the air we breathe,
    Cannot be called our own,
Still must we reap in riper years,
    The seeds in youth we've sown !

The Future ! How the spirit loves
    To dream of what may be,
To raise in air the castle walls
    Whose charm is mystery !
Past ! Present ! Future ! wond'rous three,
    Our dreams, hopes, joys are given,
To lift the soul from earthly things,
    And place our trust in Heaven.

MORDECAI.

Ahasuerus held his court,
   His courtiers serve on bended knee;
Slaves who amidst the splendor knew
   No joyous thrill that cheers the free;
The king had passed a restless night,
   For even kings have pain and care,
His gloom was mirrored in each face,
   His vassals all a shadow wear.

"Read the archives!" Prompt to obey—
   A sage the mystic scroll unrolled;
And 'neath the gleaming lamp, began
   The hidden mysteries to unfold.
He read of treason quickly quelled,
   By one who no reward received;
The king exclaimed, "Call Haman in,
   Let this omission be retrieved."

And Haman entered—nothing loth,
   The monarch's favorite had no fear.
"What shall be done to one whose deeds
   Render him worthy of our care!"
Bright shone the cruel Haman's eyes—
   "Let him the royal garment wear,
And let the chief of all thy court,
   As his attendant, greet him fair!"

" See that to Mordecai, the Jew,
    All things that thou hast said be done ;
Let no one thing omitted be
    Before the setting of the sun !"
To Mordecai, the Jew ! the man
    Who sat within the palace gate,
Who never had to Haman bowed
    With the respect due to his state,—

Who, when all others bent the knee,
    Whene'er the favorite drew nigh,
Alone retained his seat unmoved,
    Nor noticed him as he passed by !
The only blot upon the sun,
    That shone so brightly on his state,
Was this neglect of Mordecai,
    Who sat within the palace gate !

         *   *   *   *

Queen Esther made a social feast,
    And bid the king and Haman there,
No other guest met at the board—
    Esther was wise, as she was fair !
A cruel edict had gone forth,
    Her people were condemned to death,
Sadness and gloom the land pervade,
    She read the doom with bated breath

Her beauteous form she now arrayed
  In garments of humility ;
In prayer and fasting spent the time
  Until the fatal day drew nigh ;
Then she arose, and on her head,
  The golden crown her maidens placed,
With costly raiment clothed her form,
  Raiment and crown, her beauty graced !

Gently she moved—so frail, so fair—
  She leaned upon her maiden's arm,
The king is by her beauty won,
  And modesty, her chiefest charm !
" What do you seek, my gentle queen ?
  Make your request, it shall be done !"
" Bring Haman with you to the feast
  Before the setting of the sun !"

And Haman told his friends and wife,
  And gloried in his high estate,
But said : " No joy could reach his heart,
  With *Mordecai still at the gate !*"
They all exclaimed,—"A gibbet build,
  And hang the wretched Jew thereon,
Then shall you share with joy the feast
  Before the setting of the sun."

          *   *   *   *

The gloom is banished from his brow,
　The lofty gibbet rears its head.
He joins the monarch at the feast,
　The beauteous queen had spread ;
Again the king to Esther said :
　" What doth my gentle queen require ?
Full half my kingdom I will give,
　If she such gift desire !"

" My people are oppressed, O, king !
　My kinsmen are decreed to die ;
Haman—thy courtier's word can take
　Even from me, my liberty !
And Mordecai, who saved your life,
　Is doomed to hang on gibbet high ;
I do beseech my royal lord,—
　Let not my people die !"

The king was wroth and left the room,
　And Haman knelt and begged for life ;
The king exclaimed, say, " Would he force
　My beauteous queen and wife !"
Alas, for Haman no reprieve,
　From the decree that spoke his fate,
Dragged from the banquet hall, he hung
　On the high gibbet at the gate.

＊　　　＊　　　＊　　　＊

Alas! for those who, Haman like,
　　Can see no joy in life's estate,
(Though wealth and fame may be their own,)
　　With *Mordecai, still at the gate!*
The human heart is prone to ill,
　　It needs the trials life bestows;
No crown without the cross is won,
　　As all creation shows;
One single error rashly nursed,
　　One sin bewailed too late,
Has often been since Haman's days,
　　A "Mordecai within the gate!"

EVENING.

'Tis evening—and its lengthened shades
　　Are welcome to my sight;
The moon hath risen, and the stars
　　Fling round their dreamy light.

Silence hath hushed each ruder noise,
　　No sound is on the hill,
Save the soft bleating of the flocks
　　Or murmuring of the rill.

All nature sleeps, or seems to sleep,
    And peace breathes through the air
The healing balm of happiness,
    The soothing calm of prayer.

Where is the heart at this still hour
    But turns from earth to Heaven,
And humbly bows to the high power,
    To man's Redeemer given?

Who doth not wish to flee away
    From earth and all its pains,
To dwell for ever near the throne
    Where the Eternal reigns?

The lone heart now feels doubly lone,
    And sighs for that sweet rest,
Where pain and sorrow fling no more
    Their shadows o'er the blest.

The vesper-hymn like incense breathes
    Its sweetness on the air,
And earth itself is sanctified
    By evening's holy prayer.

TO-MORROW.

Time flits away on rapid wings,
    Another day hath passed,
And still "To-morrow" is the rock
    On which our hopes are cast;
The Present is the only hour
    We seem to dream away;
Vain mortal, wake! thou art not sure
    To see another day.

Swiftly each moment takes its flight,
    Lightly its track we mark,
As carelessly as those of old
    Observed the growing Ark.
Like us, "To-morrow" was their cry
    Till Time for them was past;
Awake! let us be wise to-day,
    Lest it should be our last.

The captive in his lonely cell
    Pines for the coming day;
Hope, cherub Hope! the wretch's friend,
    Smiles half his grief away;
"To-morrow" may his fetters loose,
    Once more he may be free—
Such is our state while Time is ours,
    Then comes Eternity!

Time is a treasure, use it well,
    That no remorse may cling
To bind our souls to earthly joys
    When we would upward spring.
To-day is ours—"To-morrow" may
    Behold our lifeless clay;
Then, oh my soul! be wise in time,
    Use well thy little day.

The shades of thought our souls refine
    As contemplations spring,
With rapid flight, to brighter worlds,
    Where guardian spirits sing.
The rapt soul joins the Heavenly choir
    In all their notes of joy,
As oft as Heavenly musings
    Our sinful souls employ.

Then let us every day resolve
    To bend our wayward will,
And teach our hearts the law of Him
    Who guides our wanderings still;
That when this chequered life is o'er,
    Our souls may pass away,
To realms of endless happiness,
    Where blooms Eternal Day.

NEVER DESPAIR.

Cling fast to Hope—despair is heavy armor
    That chains the soul and makes the spirit droop ;
Turn from the voice of the seducing charmer
    That tempts to evil, and cling fast to Hope !
The sunlight can illume the dreariest weather,
    Its genial beams the darkest clouds dispel ;
The moon and stars can brightly shine together,
    And cheering hope will whisper all is well.

If on life's voyage heavy tempests gather,
    And thy frail bark rocks with the boisterous gale,
Never despair !   Call on the Heavenly Father,
    Whose loving promises can never fail.
Time is the prelude to the life eternal,
    This earth the preface of the world to come,
Transient the things of time, but the supernal
    For good or evil is no fleeting doom.

" The darkest cloud may show a silver lining,"
    When the sun's rays light up the changeful sky ;
The meanest souls are those whose oft repining
    Saddens their lives and makes them fear to die.
Here we may work and bear our trials cheerly,
    Hoping when Hope itself seems anchorless.
Never despair !   Hope on and battle fairly
    For the reward that shall the victor bless.

FEBRUARY.

The rain is falling, but the showers
  Brighten "Old Winter's" hardy flowers;
The snow-drop—Flora's earliest gem,—
  Bends 'neath the breeze serene and pale,
The crocus lifts its cup of gold,
  The daffodil flaunts in the vale.
    In every corner
      The grass will be springing;
    At morn and at even
      The birds will be singing:
    "Let the winds rave,
      And call loudly for Spring,
    Still for awhile
      Old Winter is King."

The buds of the alder will soon be seen
In the dark hedge-rows, peeping between:
The snow-birds already for flight prepare,
  To colder climes and a drearier sky;
The tiny wrens again appear,
  Once more is heard the owlet's cry;

Blessed Saint Valentine's
  Votaries all,
Smiling and happy
  Respond to his call :
Mystical tidings
  Each billet-doux brings,
Sly Cupid is captive,
  And clipped are his wings.

The chains of the frost are dissolving at last,
The snow is already a dream of the past ;
On the branches where lately the icicles hung,
  The spider is busily weaving its snare ;
The squirrel abandons his wintry home,
  And the field-mouse again to its haunts doth
    repair.
      Throw off the mantle,
        Aside cast the veil,
      List to the clarion
        Notes of the gale ;
      As with the tidings
        Both hill and dale ring,
      "His *scepter*, Old Winter,
        Yields up to the Spring !"

L I F E .

Every life hath its mission,
Each moment its duty,
Every heart hath its secret,
Its care, and its cross;
In the hours of our childhood,
The season whose beauty,
We lose without feeling
The weight of our loss.

Those earliest duties,
Consist of our trying
To bear the light yoke
That inflicteth no pain;
And the loss, is the moment
So rapidly flying,
That no after repentance
Can bring back again.

First, youth—the bold rover,
So wild and romantic,
Comes bounding along
With his turbulent joys;
Making thorns for his temples,
By many an antic,
The only excuse being—
" Boys will be boys."

Next, manhood—with firm step
The gallant and steady,
Lifts up his bright eyes
To the welkin above;
His thorns, cares, and crosses,
And joys, are already
Comprised in one sentence—
"The day-dream of love."

Then age—slowly moving
Looks back on life's morning,
Or the bright days of manhood
Recalls to his mind;
The sunlight of peace
Each remembrance adorning,
With the friends that through life
Have been faithful and kind.

It is well, when our past life
Will bear retrospection;
It is well, if our duties
No shade overcast;
As we rest near the grave,
And the calmest reflection,
Consoles us when thinking
Of the days that are past.

So after the tumult,
The trials, and crosses,
And sad disappointments,
That darken our light,
The sensation of rest
Will repay all our losses,
If we trust that our crown
May be radiant and bright.

STANZAS.

Oft when the cup of life looks bright,
  The deadliest poison lurks beneath,
As meteors cast a fitful light
  And cypress with our myrtle wreath ;
Ah ! who can paint the secret tie
That binds the heart's deep sympathy ?

One—only one,—the soul can scan,
  One—only one,—can turn aside
The thorns that throng the path of man,
  Caused by his folly or his pride ;
His joys or sorrows, good or ill,
Are the soul's food or poison still.

Fate spins her tangled thread, and blends
   Our joys and woes with nicest art,
When pleasure its soft influence lends—
   Care claims some portion of the heart;
For nought on earth can perfect be,
In happiness or misery.

Bright with imagination's charms
   Is the enthralment that endears
The spirit-flame that all unharmed,
   The heart amidst its visions bears:
And wild is the entrancing flame,
And maidens blush to hear the name.

Reason in vain her beacon-light
   Flings round the shrine where fancy dwells,
The calm and holy flame burns bright,
   But that fond passion never quells,
Whose incense is the heart's pure beams,
That breathe around our own wild dreams.

The sunflower turns with ardent gaze
   Still constant to the God of Day,
And lifts its head beneath the blaze
   Of its adored divinity,
As though no other planet shone
So worthy to be gazed upon.

THE FORSAKEN.

Bright were the curls of her auburn hair,
    And fair was the cheek they shaded;
But sorrow had set its impress there,
    And the light of her eye was faded;
She took no delight in the flowers of spring,
    Though she sighed when their beauty departed,
And whispered—fit emblems are they for the tomb
    That will shelter the broken-hearted!

Oh! weep not, she said, let me pass away
    As a cloud, that one moment shaded
The bright glancing flowers of beautiful May,
    But passed ere their blossoms faded.
Oh! 'tis better to die, when a chill is thrown
    Over hopes that no more can awaken;
'Tis sweeter to die, than to feel and own,
    The blight of a heart forsaken.

I look on the future with shuddering chill,
    As a sunless track of sorrow;
And the present is tinged with forebodings of ill,
    From which I recoil with horror;
Oh! fain from this earth would my soul take wing,
    For its master-chord is breaking;
Then bring no more the flowers of spring,
    Till the grave shall hide the Forsaken.

2

DAY-DREAMS.

The first blight of sorrow is never forgot,
  'Tis the seal of the sensitive heart,
A cloud that will darken the happiest lot,
  And the last stain of earth to depart.

When sunshine and splendor illumine our way,
  'Tis a shadow that darkens life's shrine,
And amidst the wild gloom of the dreariest day
  It comes as a spell o'er the mind.

In our morning of life as we carelessly rove,
  And when joy seems the sun of our way,
If we yield to the sweet breathing whispers of love,
  And expect the bright vision to stay—

When our day-dreams are tinged with the hue of
    romance,
  And this world is a world of our own—
Oh ! 'tis sad to awake from so blissful a trance,
  And to feel ourselves doubly alone !

Ah ! what can restore us the bright hopes that threw
  Their own light o'er the things of this earth ;
Like the Planet of night, ever changing and new,
  Were the gleams that illumined our path !

'Tis painful to watch the sweet flowers as they fall
   From the wreath we so joyously wove,
And to feel that no magic on earth can recall
   The dreams that are sacred to love!

THE CLOUD.

I came into being when light was made,
   And hung o'er the garden fair,
Where man in his innocence slept in the shade,
   Creation's only heir;
And lightly I floated, overhead,
   When Eve first met his sight,
Where with roses the nuptial couch was spread,
   Shading her beauty bright.

I hung in the air when the serpent came
   To tempt with unholy lore,
The listening ear of that trembling dame,
   Who fell, to rise no more;
And I blushed with shame when her hand was
    raised,
   And to Adam the fruit was given,
And I wept when the taste by both was praised,
   That insured the loss of Heaven.

I rode through the sky, when an Angel's voice
    Called the guilty pair by name ;
That sound no more made their hearts rejoice,
    But they bent their heads with shame ;
I floated low, and their shadows fell
    On the flowers their care had nursed,
And echo returned the maddening yell
    That then from their bosoms burst.

I darkened the air, and the lightning's flash
    Leaped out from the welkin high;
When the awful thunders' pealing crash
    Was born in the inky sky ;
Again I wept when the pair began
    To till the barren ground,
I wept o'er the task of the fallen man
    When 'twas hard and rugged found.

Since then I have hung o'er the teeming earth,
    Scattering the morning dew,
Watching the flowers' bright glorious birth,
    Of every shape and hue ;
I float overhead in the mid-day sky,
    When ripens the golden grain,
And as swiftly part, when the winds are high,
    Then dissolve into drops of rain.

Beneath the rays of the moon I cower,
    And hide the stars' bright beams,
As triumphant I sail at the midnight hour
    Over mountains, rocks, and streams ;
Sometimes I appear like a vapor light,
    Then spread like a covering veil,
Till I hide the heavens from mortal sight,
    When I scatter the sounding hail.

Still I dash along ! The sunniest sky
    Is my open path by day ;
Though often like heaps of snow I lie,
    Tinged by each golden ray ;
And over the depths of the azure bright
    I sail at the noontide hour,
Then darken and shade its glorious light,
    When descends the pelting shower.

Thus at morn, mid-day, and evening hour,
    I ride through the yielding air,
Now shading the light with sovereign power,
    Now floating like zephyr fair ;
For I came into being when light was spread
    Over the teeming earth,
And shall weep over Time when he lieth dead,
    As I did at his earliest birth.

LEAP YEAR PRIVILEGE.

My name's Mrs. Catchem—I have daughters four,
  The fairest the sun shines on ;
They are pearls of price—merry and wise—
  And marriageable every one.
This being leap year, I the privilege claim
  To name them singly, and tell
The merits of each of this bevy of girls,
  And begin with my stately "Nell."

She has eyes and hair of the darkest hue,
  And skin like the Christmas snow ;
Can sing like a siren and dance like a fay,
  Untrammelled by care or woe.
At party or ball, where the fairest meet,
  She has always been voted the belle ;
Would be a fit bride for a prince or a duke—
  My winsome, beautiful "Nell."

My second daughter is gentle "Sue,"
  With hair of the sunniest brown,
And soft, shy eyes, like the violet's blue,
  And a brow never knit with a frown.
She will make a pleasant fireside dame,
  And, (under the rose be it told,)
It is *love* alone will conquer *her* heart ;
  She will never be won with gold.

The third on the list is my quiet Jane,
  Who, but for the roseate glow
Of her dimpled cheek, would be counted plain,
  As the blushes come and go.
But she is one whose lightest lay
  Can the heart with fetters bind,
And whoever shall win this dainty flower
  Will be envied by all mankind.

The fourth and last is mirthful "May,"
  The madcap who rules us all ;
Too young, as yet, for the giddy round
  Of opera, masque or ball.
Her head is crowned with nature's gift
  Of loose, dishevelled curls ;
If the truth I must tell, I love her well,
  This last of my four bright girls.

Ye who have sons will be pleased to learn
  Where we in affluence live ;
Make your choice in time, but this secret keep,
  As I know they will never forgive
The mother-love that their praises sing,
  In this auspicious year,
Address, under cover, to Mrs. C,
  Number 40 Weddington Square.

MEMORIES OF THE PAST.

The past! the past! how like a spell
　　Those words come o'er the mind,
Like the sound of distant melody
　　Upon the rushing wind.

'Tis the mantling ivy of the heart,
　　And 'neath its shade is seen
A hidden store—the retrospect
　　Of things that might have been.

The Past!　Those simple words recall
　　Full many a pleasant dream,
And many an hour of bitterness
　　In life's uncertain stream.

The rosy hopes of early days,
　　Too transient to last,
And the chill of heart that first was known
　　Are memories of the Past.

The hearth where happy faces smiled,
　　In the home of early years,
The gay companions of our youth,
　　Ere the cheek was stained with tears.

The schoolmate friend, our earliest love
  Remembered first and last ;
The trysting-tree, where once we met,
  Are memories of the past.

THE IRISH EMIGRANT.

Mournfully the harp of Old Erin
  Sounds o'er the sad sea waves ;
We listen, expecting blithe music,
  We hear but the dirge of its graves.
No longer the laugh of the Banshee
  Blends with the sweet summer gale,
But the sigh of the emigrant leaving
  His home in Avoca's fair vale.

Dark is the pathway before him,
  And lonely his exile will be,
His home and his birthplace behind him,
  His babe on its fair mother's knee ;
Oppression his footsteps has driven
  From the faces so patient and mild,
His labor no longer sufficient
  To earn food for mother and child.

2*

Abandoned the home of his fathers,
　　The Green Island girt by the sea,
For the land of the forest and prairie,
　　" The home of the brave and the free !"
He loves the hoarse roar of the ocean,
　　Every leaf of the Shamrock is dear,
And amidst his sad heart's fond emotion,
　　From his pale cheek he dashes the tear.

Hope points to a cottage and homestead,
　　Where the vine and the roses entwine,
And Faith cheers the heart of the exile,
　　And whispers, " both soon shall be thine."
Now cheerly he wakens the echoes,
　　That slumbering hide in the caves,
Calmly bidding, Farewell, to Old Erin,
　　Its mountains, fields, valleys, and waves.

MARCH.

As a school-boy in his glee,
Enters March right merrily ;
In his hands are winds and sleet,
The snow is clinging to his feet,
Passing by the breezy hill,
He whistles with a right good will.
The sun dissolves the ice and snow,
Again the ice-bound waters flow ;
On the tree the robin swings,
And the Spring's first anthem sings,
As his cheerful notes are heard,
Answers every forest bird,
Who in their haunts again are seen,
Ere the alder's shoots are green.
The modest primrose loves the shade,
Where the black-bird's nest is made ;
Close beside the daffodil
Is nodding to the murmuring rill ;
In the cultured garden bed,
The snowdrop lifts its crystal head,
And the crocus' cups of gold,
The early dew-drops gently hold.

As the days are brighter seen,
The daisy gems the meadow green,
The buttercup, and celandine,
Also in the meadows shine;
Whilst hidden in the hedge-row near,
The purple violet scents the air,
Humble flowers,—but first to bring,.
Their offering to the welcome Spring.

Loud and shrill the March winds blow,
Clearing from the earth the snow,
The rain descends in pelting showers,
Calling to the trees and flowers,
" Put forth your shoots, your incense bring
To hail the advent of the Spring."

THE SNOWDROP.

All hail ! to the firstling of the year,
With slender stem and blossoms fair !
It tells that old winter is passing away,
That spring is approaching with flowerets gay.
The clouds will scatter April showers,
To moisten the earth and freshen the flowers,
The robin will chant from the budding thorn
Its matin song at earliest dawn,
And waken the woodland choristers all
To join in Nature's festival.

No guardian leaves uphold the gem,
First star in Flora's diadem ;
Yet bravely it bears the bitter blast,
And sweetly smiles when the storm is past.
Like faith it lifts its head on high,
It bends—not breaks—as winds sweep by,
Sheds radiance on the lowliest ground
As its gentle glories gleam around ;
Then hail, all hail ! to the tiny thing,
That heralds the coming of lovely spring !

OLD SONGS.

The mariner keeps his midnight watch
   As the stately ship sails on,
And whistles the tunes of his native land
   He no longer can gaze upon:
Old Songs! that tell of moor and fell;
   Of forest, mountain and plain;
Of home, and friends, and fireside joys,
   And the wild waves sing the refrain.
Old Songs! how your sounds on land or sea
   Thrill the heart with pleasure or woe,
And mantle the cheek or bedew the eye
   With the memories of long ago.

The farmer as he follows the plow,
   Or scatters the golden grain,
With the merry lark warbling over head,
   Sings songs of the rolling main:
Of the gallant seaman tempest-tossed,
   And the loud winds wailing cry,
Till in spirit he stands on the lonely deck
   And lists to the surges sigh.
Old Songs! how your sounds on land or sea
   Thrill the heart with pleasure or woe,
And mantle the cheek or bedew the eye
   With the memories of long ago.

The soldier after a toilsome march,
　As he raises his sheltering tent,
Or rests on the sward, by his comrade's side,
　To his joys and griefs gives vent
By singing old songs of home and friends,
　Fertile fields and flowerets gay,
And heartily drinks from his canteen cup
　A health to those far away.
Old Songs ! how your sounds on land or sea
　Thrill the heart with joy or woe,
And mantle the cheek or bedew the eye
　With the memories of long ago.

Old Songs ! what magic is in the words
　That drive away dull care,
As memory turns to the joyful past,
　When life was bright and fair.
The songs we sung at our mother's knee,
　Though the humblest of humble lays,
Will now often dim our eyes with tears
　In remembrance of happier days.
Old Songs ! how your sounds on land or sea
　Thrill the heart with pleasure or woe,
And mantle the cheek or bedew the eye
　With the memories of long ago.

"NEVER GIVE UP."

Let us never give up! amidst trials and crosses
    That man in all stations is called to sustain,
In the battle of life,—to keep counting our losses
    Will certainly bring us an increase of pain ;
Let the breast-plate of Truth remain bright as a
      mirror,
    As the tiniest speck will diminish its rays,
If a shadow pass over its surface, remember
    To remove the dark shade, will redound to our
      praise.

Let us never give up! if we now and then falter,
    Let us rise on the instant and never despair ;
There is always the refuge of God's Holy Altar,
    And our blessed Redeemer awaiting us there ;
Take the helmet of Faith, let it shine on our temples,
    Let the buckler of Hope brace our arm for the strife,
And let the bright mantle of Charity cover
    Every word, every wish, and design of our life.

Let us never give up! there are moments whose
      brightness
    Will repay all the labor the diligent brave ;
A heart that despairs will at once lose its lightness,
    He who carries the fetters,—resembles the slave ;
He who wins in the race,—is not always the fleetest,
    The victor in battle,—not always the strong,
But to him who endures to the end, persevering
    In the strife and the combat, the prize shall belong.

Let us never give up! they who wrought for one
    hour,
In the vineyard of God, were rewarded the same,
As the few faithful souls, bearing sunshine and
    shower,
So well, that their lives were not subject to blame;
When we hear of the mansions too numerous to
    mention,
In the city of God, whose bright flowers are the
    skies,
Our trials, afflictions, and crosses, appear far
    Too light for our tears, and too brief for our sighs.

FLOWERS.

"Man's days are as grass,—as the flowers of the field so shall
he flourish."

Bring flowers,—bright flowers,—for the young and
    fair,
To twine 'midst the waves of their sunny hair,
    On this their festival day!
Go search for the primrose, in leafy dell,
The violet,—the cowslip,—and lily-bell,
    And beautiful sprigs of May.

To deck the fair bride, bring the orange flower,
That alone must be worn at the nuptial hour,
  When the vows of faith are given;
Meet emblem, it seems, of the mystical sway
That shall bind two hearts in one this day,
  On their after path to Heaven.

For the burial ground,—bring the mournful yew,
The rose-mary,—cypress,—thyme, and rue, .
  And pansies of every shade;
The suthern-wood green, with its feathery leaves
And the marigold fair, may adorn the graves
  Where the sacred dead are laid.

These beautiful things have a meaning high
Though they only blossom to fade and die
  Like human life at best;
At morn we are nursed with a mother's care,
At noon, own a tie more sacred and dear,
  And at evening sink to rest!

Then gather ye flowers of every hue,
The rose-bud, orchis, and hare-bell blue,
  To mark the fleeting hours;
Like them we may flaunt our little span,
For to *bloom* and *die* is ordained unto man,
  As well as to plants and flowers!

THE LEGEND OF DISMAS.

A FRAGMENTARY TRADITION.

Herod on his throne turned pale
As he listened to the WISE MEN's tale,
That a star had risen in the sky
To mark the spot where the babe should lie:
That they had left their Father-land,
Impelled by a Divine command
To worship where the young child lay,
And to Him kingly honors pay.

He asked their purposed route of them,
Their answer was,—to "BETHLEHEM!"
"Proceed," he cried, "and when you find
The babe to wear a crown designed,
Let me too know, that I may raise
My voice with yours in prayer and praise,
As I shall not to bow refuse
Before the young King of the Jews,"

They parted. He to call his guards,
To whom he promised large rewards
When every child of tender age
Should die, to quell his frantic rage.
The Wise Men in a manger found,
With swaddling bands securely bound,
A weeping babe :—yet low they bowed,
And His high lineage breathed aloud.

Their frankincense and gold they cast
On the stable floor. Then tears fell fast,
And heartfelt prayers and sighs they pour
As they knelt the Infant King before.
They thought not of the humble shed,
But bent beside the lowly bed,
And loud proclaimed their zeal and joy,
Devoid of fear or doubt's alloy.

His virgin-mother, fair and good,
And foster-father, weeping stood,
And humble shepherds knelt around
With joy, that they their God had found !
Cold was the night when Christ was born,
For our sakes, of His glory shorn,
He came on earth to bleed and die,
That we might live eternally.

And did the Kings retrace the track
That led to cruel Herod back?
No! warned by God of his intent,
Home by another path they went.
Rage filled the tyrant's cruel mind,
To all but fury madly blind;
He doomed the Innocents to die,—
But Christ escaped the massacre.

*　　*　　*　　*　　*　　*

Cold, dark, and drear, was the winter night,
When child and mother took their flight;
An old man was their guide and stay,
But God doth watch their onward way:—

Mary's face was wondrous fair,
Love and joy were beaming there,
She soothed the Infant at her breast,
And hushed His plaintive cries to rest:
St. Joseph, with his staff in hand,
Was earthly guide to the humble band:
—Thus the pilgrimage begun
On earth, of God's eternal Son!

*　　*　　*　　*　　*　　*

"Stand!" said a voice to the humble band,
"Halt, or ye die!   I command ye stand!"
Bright flashed the sabres of armed men,
Who had sprung to their feet from a rocky glen;
"Give us your gold, or ye surely shall die,"
"As no one unscathed shall pass us by."

There stood the Virgin, the Son, the Sire,
With naught to allay the fierce men's ire;
Life you may take, our blood you may spill,
We humbly bow to God's Holy Will!
Gold we have none, we are poor and mean,
GOD is the rampart on which we lean!

Their looks of love, and words had power
To turn the evil in that dark hour;
One, who appeared supreme in command,
Quickly dismissed the frowning band.

Beauty and Innocence, gifts divine,
Thousands have bowed at your holy shrine;
Man in his darkest, deadliest mood,
Hath often been quelled by the truly good;
There is in Virtue a powerful spell,
A charm, whose strength all rage can quell.

He who had hearts, and ready hands,
To fulfil, without murmur, his high commands,
Who ruled like a King in that wild domain,
Turned to that humble group again.

Pale was the cheek of the lowly maid,
Who looked but to Heaven for instant aid,
Soft was the glance of her radiant eyes
To the spot where her Infant in slumber lies,
So lately, she saw the three Kings kneel,
And homage pay with ardent zeal,
So lately, she saw the shepherds bend,
And heard their prayers to heaven ascend,
That she looked at the babe, and felt no fear,
No sense of danger while HE was there!
She thought of the Angel's holy " HAIL !"
Of the word of God that could not fail,
That her Son should reign on David's throne,
And she felt not afraid, though they stood alone.
St. Joseph gazed on her gentle face,
And caught the fervor of Holy grace!
'Twas an Angel's voice that bid them roam,
That bid him seek in Egypt a home;
An Angel who bid him nothing fear,
But make the Child his especial care :—
So he raised his heart to Heaven's throne,
And prayed for help from the Holy One !

The Babe had sunk in peaceful rest,
Like a young bird in its summer nest;
He, who could ride the whirlwind wild,
Had taken the semblance of a child;
He, who could bid the tempest cease,
The troubled waters flow in peace,
Now seemed to wait the wayward will
Of that robber fierce to save or kill!
He left his throne in Heaven above,
To prove for sinful man his love,
And ere he again ascended the sky,
He knew for man he must bleed and die;
But he knew a weary and painful way,
Ere that day should dawn, before him lay;
He seemed like an Infant helpless and fair,
The object of Joseph and Mary's care!

*   *   *   *   *   *   *

"There is a power that guards thy way,
Thou art safe from harm, I cannot slay.
I cannot touch one single hair,
That lays on the brow of that Infant fair;
Nor can I harm thee, thou aged man,
Still less that Lady, so pale and wan;
But I can guard your steps, and keep
Watch round your couch, while in safety you sleep.
None in this wilderness, wild though it be,
Whilst I am your friend, will injure ye!

" Here feelings of pity are seldom shown,
And acts of compassion less seldom known,
Tears on my cheeks have ceased to flow,
So much have I witnessed of human woe ;
This chill at my heart is a fearful guest,
Ye are free to depart,—or here to rest."

* * * * * * *

The noon-day sun on Calvary's height,
Looked down with a dull and lurid light ;
Pilate sat in the Judgment-seat,
And the Son of Man, stood at his feet
Pinioned and bound, reviled and sold,
By one of the Twelve, for love of gold ;
Pilate felt sad and inclined to spare,
For his wife had begged with earnest prayer,
That he from Innocent blood that day
Would withhold his hand,—nor the Just man slay.
But wild was the noise of the lawless crew,
As shout after shout still louder grew,
No cause could be found why he should die,
—" Let him be Crucified," was their cry !

Little they knew, when their fiendish cry
Ascended from earth to the vaulted sky,
When they, in their rage, for vengeance cried,
Of the fall that awaited their towering pride :
3

Full little they knew that he who stands
Bound like a felon, with many bands,
Whose voice is so meek and lowly there,
Whose brow the thorny crown doth wear,
To whom with scorn, they have bent the knee
And cried " ALL HAIL !" in mockery;
Who hath been smitten, and bid to speak
Whose hand it was, that struck his cheek;
Little, ah ! little, they knew His power,
Tho' reviled and outraged in that dark hour.

*   *   *   *   *   *

Oh ! Sin, whose venom found its way
Even to Eden's garden gay,
Whose power to check, whose rod to break,
JESUS is humbled, mild and meek !
Never, oh ! never, since Adam fell,
Was Satan so powerful out of Hell,
He felt some unknown mystery grew
Around that Man,—whose birth he knew
Was lowly.   He saw his mother mild
When she brought forth the weeping child,
And deemed St. Joseph was his sire,—
Therefore he frowned with hellish ire,
When at the manger, lowly and bare,
The Wise Men knelt to creation's heir !
Ah ! worship, he cried, that puling thing,
Exult and proclaim him Heaven's King,
Spread out your gifts and bow the knee,
For God will punish such mockery.

When the child to manhood grew,
Still tortured, he kept his form in view;
When in the wilds he stood alone,
He offered to Him an earthly throne,
And turned abashed from the wondrous sway,
That crushed his power in the open day;
Now, that again, alone he stands
Awaiting his doom from unpitying hands,
Satan, outrageous, among the crew
His power exerted, and venom threw.

Rage filled the breast of these fallen men,
"Shall he be King!" they exclaim again,
" Let him but die, no King have we
" But Cæsar!   To him we will bow the knee!
" Release us, Barabbas!   Away, away,
" Let him bleed and die, ere the close of day!"

*   *   *   *   *   *

Three Crosses are raised on Calvary's height,
On each hangs a form in woful plight,
Naked, and bound, to the rugged tree,
Each in extremest agony.

The One in the midst, in his hand hath borne
A reed for a sceptre—and also hath worn
The thorny crown around his brow,
From which the innocent blood doth flów;
To Him, in scorn, the eager crowd
Words of homage breathed aloud :—
" Father," he cried, with tears of woe,
" Forgive them, they know not what they do !"

One of the thieves, with bitterness,
Seeking to add to his deep distress,—
" If thou art the Son of God," said he,
" Command that I 'scape this cursed tree,"
" Save thyself, too, from these painful bands,
" That we may escape their detested hands."

" Peace," said the other with penitent tone,
" Respect the woes of this Holy One,
We, for our crimes, deserve this death,
'Tis fearful to blaspheme with dying breath,
Rail not at justice, but let us die
In peace with all men 'neath the sky."
Then, turning to Jesus, he loudly cried,
(While the other His power as loudly defied,)
" Remember me, Lord, at the Judgment-seat,
When before the Eternal, we two shall meet !"

Oh ! for a seraph's glowing fire,
 An Angel's holy love,
To paint the joys that filled his soul
 Descending from above,
As these words of Christ fell on his ear
 " This day thou shalt be, with me,
In Paradise," that blissful sphere,
 From pain and suffering free !

  * * * * * *

What is there in that gentle tone,
That recalls to memory scenes long flown ?
Why does he blend with that bleeding form
A being of beauty, bright and warm ?
An aged man, and sleeping child,
That he once preserved in a desert wild ?
Why like a spell doth he seem to stand
Again on the spot, where his frowning band
Were dismissed—that an Infant might cherished be
In the earliest bloom of its infancy ?
Once more the chill at his heart he feels,
And earth, and heaven, before him reels ;
There stands the Lady so pale and fair,
That then he made his especial care,
More sad and pale, more holy and pure,
From the woes that now she doth endure.

Weeping beneath the Cross she stands
With upraised face, and clasped hands,
Her soul is torn, her brain is sear,
Never before was that form so dear,
Friends might forsake, and apostles fly,
And traitors might scoff at his agony,
Disciples might fear—but a mother's love
Will rise all earthly cares above !

So every pang, that his soul had riven,
Was doubled in hers.   She would have given
Her all on earth to have kissed his cheek,—
Still her grief was silent, she could not speak ;
Spell-like she gazed on that blood-stained brow,
Whilst fast her sorrowful tears did flow !

*   *   *   *

Again the voice of Jesus stole,
Over the listening robber's soul ;
" Woman," it said, " Behold thy Son !"
Then again to a dear loved one,
" Son, behold thy Mother," he cried,
Then meekly bowed his head and died !

And as escaped that parting breath,
Man was redeemed from Eternal Death,
The power of Satan was circumscribed
By the blood, that the Cross of our Saviour dyed !

*   *   *   *

Dark grew the Heavens, the rocks were rent,
And the bodies that long had in earth been pent,
Arose from their graves :—the lightnings' flash
Replied to the deep-mouthed thunder's crash ;
Never before had earth and sky
Been so discomposed since Eternity.
The veil of the Temple was rent in twain,
And trembling sinners howled with pain,
They beat their breasts, and tore their hair,
And called upon death in their despair !
Mixed with the tempests awful breath,
Uprose their harrowing shrieks for death !
Oh ! God, it was dreadful to hear their cries
Blend with the wrath of the angry skies ;
To feel the gloom of that deepest night,
While round the Cross gleamed a glorious light ;
'Twas awful to know the dead had risen,
So long entombed in their earthly prison ;
To hear the crash of the Temple's veil,
To list to the sound of the echoing gale
All, all was terrible,—but the worst
To endure, was the thought of these men accursed !

*   *   *   *

Where shall now the scoffer hide,
Where is uplifted the brow of pride,
Where are the knees in mockery bowed,
The tongues, that curses have breathed aloud,
Where are the hands that dealt the blow,
The hearts,—that exulted in Jesu's woe,
Where, oh! where, in this terrible hour,
Shall they hide from Conscience's mystic power?

——Conscience, that angel of calm content,
When memory points to a life well spent;
Conscience, that fiend which no spell can lay
When we from the path of duty stray:
Conscience, the soother when most distrest,
The foretaste of joys that awaits the blest:
Or, when defiled, the deepest thorn,
That can by erring man be worn:
The string that trembles in softest light,
That renders darker, the blackest night:
That stills the sigh of the martyr's soul,
And alone, our destinies can control!

* * * *

What were the pangs of those outcast few,
That the blood of a suffering Saviour drew,
To the doom eternal that waits the hour,
When Satan shall over their souls have power?
When mercy no more can relieve their pain,
And even the blood of the Saviour be vain
To plead for them?—Oh! God, to think
Of the horror that lurks on Hell's terrible brink,
Of the ruin,—the misery,—that awaits
The souls that shall pass those burning gates,
Those who have scorned a Saviour's love,
Slighted eternal joys above,
To gratify passions low and base,
The love of gold, or the vile embrace
Of venal forms; the glittering cheer,
Or the tottering, feeble, drunkard's leer,
The desire of gain, that knows no bounds,—
All these have slighted Christ's bleeding wounds,
Rendered His death and sufferings vain
And thereby Him crucified over again!

* * * *

3*

Amidst the tumult that raged around,
Above, below, and underground,
Amidst the curses that filled the air,
Lightly uprose one voice in prayer ;
Close by the bleeding Saviour's side
By felon bands securely tied,
To a rugged cross, hung the robber wild
Who had succored Jesus when a child !

There was one spot in memory's track
On which with joy he could still look back,
Amidst scenes of blood it threw its light,
Though all else was dark, it still shone bright ;
He had shown mercy, and now received
Assurance that he was reprieved ;
In the darkest hour of his fell career,
This act of pity shone brightly there.

Condemned, and raised 'twixt Heaven and earth,
Calmly the ransomed drew his breath,
Clung to the promise Jesus gave,
Hoped through His death, his soul to save.
Hard was the bed on which he died,
But the Son of Man hung by his side,—
And he looked on the wounds of his suffering Lord,
Till he felt not the tightness of the cord !

    He died as all would wish to die,—
    In the hope of a happy Eternity !

     *   *   *   *   *

APRIL.

Month of smiles and showers,
Changeful skies, and flowers,
   Hither, hither come!
I have wooed thee long,
These woodland scenes among,—
   Hasten to thy home.

Scatter from thy hand,
Upon the teeming land,
   Garlands fresh and fair :
Call the swallows back,
From their pathless track,
   To meet thee here.

Thou ridest on the gale,
And the lily, pale,
   Uprears its head ;
Let thy dew-drops lie
Beneath the changeful sky,
   Where Flora's couch is spread.

The cuckoo's voice is clear,
And to the listening ear,
      Bright promise brings—
Of flowerets wild and free,
To whom the wandering bee
      Its welcome sings.

The rook builds in the wood,
And rears its sable brood
      Secure on high :
The lark from upland springs,
And loud its carol rings,
      Ascending to the sky.

Sweet month, we bid thee hail !
The winter's coat of mail
      No more is seen,—
But on the flowery lea,
And on the budding tree,
      Fresh shoots of green.

Oh ! we shall miss thy tears
When fragrant May appears,
      Then, fare thee well !
The birds at early dawn,
Upon the budding thorn,
      Shall sing thy knell !

THE EVENING PRIMROSE.

Little floweret, pure and pale,
Thy scent rides on the evening gale
    At twilight's holy hour,
Within the coppice thou art found,
Like gems upon enchanted ground,
    Around each vernal bower.

The flaunting daffodil is seen
Amidst its leaves of deepest green,
    To shut at close of day ;
And though the violet loves the shade,
It sleeps when day's bright glories fade,
    Beneath the fragrant May.

Thou only, when the western star
Sheds its mild radiance from afar,
    Canst gaze upon its beams.
Sweet little floweret, bright and gay,
Thy leaves expand at close of day
    Like Hope's fantastic dreams.

Upon the hill and in the vale,
Thou lifts thy cup, serene and pale,
    To sip the dewdrops bright ;
Thy bloom unseen by mortal eyes,
Bursts into life, expands and dies
    Beneath the silent night.

Here, let Ambition learn to bear
The maddening throes of fell despair,
  When all its schemes shall fail;
Learn Resignation from thy form,
That shrinks not from the gathering storm,
  Or rushing evening gale.

THE HERALDS OF SPRING.

Again the little snow-drops
 Hang down their pearly heads,
Adorning with their purity
 The garden's rugged beds.
No shade or stain of earth appears
 Upon these lowly flowers,
The earliest stars that nature flings
 Upon this earth of ours.
Like to the smiles of childhood,
 When sadness chills the brow,
Amidst their spear-like leaves they raise
 Their glorious bells of snow.

The snow-wreath on the hill-tops
   Defies the sun's mild rays,
The birds within the wild-wood
   Thrill forth their hymns of praise,
The evergreens look brighter
   With the dew-drops on their leaves,
And the robin for the hedge-row
   Forsakes the cottage eaves;
He leaves us when the daisies,
   Amidst the emerald green
That is springing up around us,
   Looking up to Heaven, are seen.

The snow-drop in the garden-bed,
   The daisy on the lea,
The music from the leafless trees,
   The green grass wild and free,
They all proclaim that winter,
   Cold winter must depart,
And that Spring, with buds and blossoms,
   Will bring gladness to the heart.
Come forth from town and city,
   Make the woodland echoes ring
With a song for the fair snow-drops,
   The harbingers of spring.

HOPE.

Bright Spirit, oh ! where is thy place of rest,
What home of this earth dost thou love the best?
Are the shrines in which thou lovest to lie,
The hearts that rejoice when thy step is nigh?
Are the smiles that beam on the lips' sweet red,
Thy resting place, thy fragrant bed ;
Or, are the trembling tears thy prize,
That gently fall from beauty's eyes?

Hearts have their deep felt thrill of pain !
It is not there thou wouldst wish to reign ;
Smiles are too frequently followed by sighs
For them to be thy sacrifice !
There are tears of joy as well as woe ;
Bright are the drops that glittering flow :
But thou canst not wear 'midst thy locks of light,
Gems on which sorrow hath cast its blight !

I have watched thy track with a votary's flame,
As in lonely moments to me you came ;
And paid deep worship, as thy soothing power
Hath chased the clouds of my darker hour ;
But I could not find the mystic sway
To bind thy glittering pinions gay ;
Ere the first bright light of thy smile was past
Care had again its shadows cast.

Midst the stars thou hast hung thy glowing wreath,
That no stain of earth may near it breathe ;
And thou pointest up to Heaven's sphere,
As one who hath but a *mission* here.
Oh ! may my heart like thine arise,
On thy Spirit's track to thy native skies,
And the homage pay, thou lovest to twine,
Mid thy starry wreath on thy brow divine !

THE BATTLE OF LIFE.

The seasons come, and the seasons go,
    The past has a far-off look alway,
So little success in what we do,
    When our arms are weak and our hair is gray.
To-day we feel the chilling blast,
    That we quaffed like wine in the long ago ;
Oh ! that the joy of spring would cast
    Its charming beams o'er our winter's snow.

In youth what dreams of fame and power
    We revel in ;—when the world is new
What plans we make to improve each hour,
    When every pulse of the heart beats true !

Life, in itself, is so glad a boon,
    As our hearts expand to its wayward schemes,
Bright as the rays of the silver moon
    That glisten on mountains, rocks, and streams.

At noon, we rested, not taking heed
    Of the fleeting moments' rapid flight;
In age, they pass with double speed,
    As we feel the shade of the coming night.

So little done—to redeem the past,
    With lifted hand we kneel and pray,
As the shipwrecked mariner clings to the mast—
    Unheeded we pass from this earth away.

We bury the dead in the dull, cold earth
    Silent and lonely their dreamless sleep,
The world, as usual, teems with mirth,
    Forgetting the mourners who sadly weep.

And this, the reward for days and years,
    So freely given to foes and friends,
The loss is scarcely worth our tears,
    The grave is the goal where our journey ends.

THE GUARDIAN ANGEL.

As night follows day, the roseate morn
Dispels the dark gloom at earliest dawn,
Lightly the clouds pass to and fro,
Veiling the sun from the earth below,
Till again the moon, Queen regent of night,
Gladdens the earth with her silver light;
The dark mists rest on the mountain's crown,
Whose steeps are clothed with heather brown;
The pearly tears of the dewdrops fall,
With grief for the flowers withered all;
The rich soil nurtures the ripening grain,
Though crushed by the wind and falling rain;
The bulrushes grow in the sluggish mere,
All in their meet and appointed sphere,
And the years pass onward silently,
Till Time gives place to Eternity.

A helpless babe to the earth is given,
Whose heritage is a throne in Heaven;
Whether lowly born or of high degree,
Its future is veiled in mystery.
Life is a warfare from the first,
And the innocent babe, by its mother nursed,
Whose kisses are pressed on cheek and brow,
Oft in the future may work her woe.

Two spirits keep watch o'er its steps alway,
One as bright as the sun by day,
The other as dark as the midnight hour,
When storms are rife and the tempests lower.
The beautiful Angel its steps attend,
Unseen and unnoticed, yet still its friend ;
But with the first stain on its youthful mind,
The Spirit of Evil its chains can bind.

Life hath its moments of joy and woe,
Its trials and crosses here below ;
Even childhood is not exempt from pain,
As all are born with a transient stain ;
And as our years so our cares increase,
Sometimes war and sometimes peace ;
Every step we take is toward "that bourne
From which no traveler can return."
How bright are the visions of early youth,
When our loins are girded with zeal and truth ;
So when years increase and the mystic tree,
Of Good and Evil we clearly see,
'Tis well if our actions, by day and night,
Keep by our side "the Angel bright,"
Till closing in Death our mortal eyes,
He may joyfully herald us to the skies.

REMEMBER ME.

When you wander forth alone,
   And the shades of evening fall,
With their fitful, shadowy gloom,
   O'er creation like a pall ;
When the stars are seen above,
   And the fire-fly on the lea,
Like the meteor flame of love,
   Oh ! then remember me !

When joy is breathing near thee,
   A light and dulcet strain,
When sorrow doth not spare thee,
   Its deep-felt thrill of pain ;
In thy hours of social gladness,
   When thy soul is full of glee,
In thy lonely hours of sadness,
   Oh ! then remember me !

I shall think of thee at even,
   When the memories of the past,
Like the pilgrim's dreams of Heaven
   Come thronging wild and fast ;
I shall watch thy favorite Planet
   In its pure unclouded flight,
And shall fancy thou art gazing
   On the splendor of its light.

THE EMIGRANT'S SONG.

I dreamt of home in a foreign land
    Beneath the elm-trees' shade,
When the scorching rays of the noon-day sun
    'Midst its quivering branches played ;
Of my childhood's home, by the mountain's brow,
    With its waters bright and clear,
And the mingled voices of those I loved,
    As in days of yore were there.

Of home ! and once again I heard
    The notes of the mountain band,
And mixed in the sunset sports of those
    I had known in my native land ;
The vision fled, and my soul was sad,
    For I felt that my lot was lone,
And I sighed for the friends of early life
    And the joys of my native home.

Oh, sleep ! how kindly are the smiles
    Thou showest on faces dear,
How sweet are the tones of the loved one's voice
    As they steal on the dreamer's ear ;
Life hath its sad realities,
    Its cold and heartless schemes,
But the spirit loves the gleams of light
    That visit our joyous dreams.

WELCOME TO SPRING.

Already the hawthorn with vesture of green,
And buds of white May, by the roadside are seen,
Already the violet gleams on the wolds,
And the evening primrose its leaves unfolds,
The daffodil bends on its tender stem,
And the daisy is seen like a household gem,
Breathing of gladness, on mountain and plain,
That Spring hath arisen on earth again.

The snow hath dissolved on the sunny hills,
And the ice no longer confines the rills,
This is the season when bird and bee,
Are pouring forth sounds of liberty ;
High on the pine, rocks the sable rook,
And the minnow is seen in the rippling brook,
The robin forsakes the cottagers' door,
Where so lately he shared their frugal store.

All Nature is gay ! the lowliest thorn
Is bright with the gems of the roseate morn ;
Mixed with the winds, comes the breath of flowers,
The birds are at work in the leafy bowers,
Building their nests with nicest skill ;
And the emmets are busy on every hill ;
The bees are abroad on lightsome wing,—
Who would not rejoice in the time of Spring ?

Why does the floweret deck the ground,
Why are the green leaves bursting around,
Why do the songs of the bird and bee,
Blend in one chorus of melody?
Is it not,—that the human heart,
May bear in the general joy its part?
May join the mute homage of leaf and flower,
And meekly the God of nature adore?

THE VIOLET.

In girlhood I sought thee, thou sweet-scented flower,
To bloom on my bosom, and plant round my bower;
I sought thee in springtime, when tempted to rove,
To list to the cushet in each shady grove,
And my young heart beat wildly when shaking the
    dew
From the green of thy leaves or thy blossoms so blue.

I sought thee to wreathe with the primrose so pale,
The white blossomed May, or that pride of the vale,
The snowy-robed lily, with glistening bells,
Where the busy bee gathered the sweet for its cells;
I knew where the meek little celandine grew,
But dearly I loved thee, thou floweret of blue.

The starry-eyed daisy I sought on the lea,
The bright daffodil and the cowslip so free,
And that gem of the meadow, the butter-cup wild,
I gathered with joy when a young playful child;
But thy blossom, sweet floweret retiring and coy,
Brings yet to my heart its full measure of joy.

THE MOON.

Resplendent she maketh the night,
    Looking down upon mountain and plain,
The rivers reflecting her light,
    And the waves of the turbulent main;
Every cycle she newly appears,
    Like a crescent of gold in the sky,
Dispelling the vaporous clouds
    That appear o'er her surface to fly.

Resplendent she maketh the eve,
    Rising upwards and higher alway,
As the leaflets the dew-drops receive,
    Like tears at the close of the day.
The sun hides his beams in the sea,
    And as his refulgence grows dim,
She appeareth surrounded by clouds,
    But alas! no companion for him.
4

Resplendent she maketh the morn,
　　And ruleth the tides of the seas ;
Now gilding the ripening corn,
　　Now silvering the leaves of the trees ;
The owl and the bat circle round,
　　And the mocking-bird sings in the shade,
Making vocal the solitude sweet
　　Of the deepening forest arcade.

She is lonely—the stars have their peers,
　　And silent—no planet so pale,
No music her solitude cheers,
　　Save the echoing blast of the gale ;
The homage the starry host yields,
　　The perfumes from earth that arise
But slightly atone for the loss
　　Of the glittering sun from the skies.

When she rises the stars are outshone,
　　And when veiled by the clouds is her light,
The twinkling orbs sadly look on,
　　As at times she is hidden from sight ;
The water reflecteth her face,
　　Every wavelet looks up to the sky,
As shining on river and lake,
　　The winds sing her soft lullaby.

MAY.

Hark to the musical choir in the woodlands,
  List to the warbling of each tuneful lay;
What are the leaves and the bright blossoms saying,
  To welcome the dawning of beautiful May?

Every fresh floweret its incense is offering,
  Tossing the dew-drops from chalice and leaf,
The birds to the sunbeams their joyous notes trill-
      ing,
    Sincere in their rapture, though transient and
      brief.

Brightly the waters are rippling and dancing,
  Swiftly the finny tribe circle and leap,
Hoarsely the waves of old Ocean are chiming,
  Scattering the pebbles tossed up by the deep.

To the base of the rocks the seaweed is clinging,
  The shells of the ocean gleam white on the shore,
The outward bound mariner, the maintop is climb-
      ing,
    To gaze on the land he may never see more.

Long ago on this morning, the youths and the
      maidens
    Selected a May Queen, the fairest and best,
And all day held revel on the green round the
      May-pole
    With song, rustic dance, and innocent jest.

High homage was paid to this Queen of an hour,
   Who ruled o'er her subjects with absolute sway,
Whilst the aged looked on, and remembered the
    season,
   When they in Old Times, hailed the Queen of
    May.

Oh! land of my birth, thy hills and thy valleys,
   Thy mountains, and plains, are no longer my
    home,
Yet my heart fondly dwells on thy innocent pas-
    times,
   And I love thee more dearly the farther I roam.

To me, on this morning, the blossoms and flowers,
   The ocean, and song-birds, one madrigal sing,
And I turn from the present, its cares and its trials,
   In spirit to join in thy welcome to Spring.

A MYSTERY.

I wonder if over the dark blue sea,
My ship will ever return to me?
I look on the waves as they ripple and flow;
Now sullen and dark, now white as snow,
On the rocky beach, on the pebbly shore,
And list to the tempest's deafening roar;
I look on the starry host at even,
Twinkling like watchfires lit in Heaven;

I gaze on the golden orb of day,
I watch the moon on its onward way,
I people the earth with spirits of grace
That always look on the Father's face!
The bursting to life of weed and flower
Give proof to my heart of His infinite power!
All nature is veiled in mystery,
And my ship is far, far out at sea.

I launched my ship when life was new,
And placed her in charge of the good and true;
I freighted her hold in every part
With the sunniest hopes of the human heart;
At the helm I placed, with rudder in hand,
The virgin Hope.   When in sight of land
I spread the sails with fervent prayers,
And sprinkled the deck with pity's tears.
With the cordage of Faith, securely fast,
And trimly tackled each spar and mast;
And the pure white sails that fluttered free
Were woven by gentle Charity.
The demon Fear no room could find
In warp or weft his chains to bind;
I bid my ship "God-speed" o'er the sea—
Ah! will she ever return to me?

Many days and nights have, uncounted, passed by,
And long ago I have learned to sigh;
Amidst my hopes there have mingled fears,
Smiles have been mixed with heartfelt tears;
Frequent and oft from the freighted hold
The cargo has been unloaded and sold;
But alas! the realized price was low,
For the market was overstocked long ago.
Hope at the helm undaunted hath stood,
And the coils and ropes of Faith are good;
Charity yet spreads her fluttering sails
To catch the breezes of varying gales;
From the deck the sun hath drank up the tears
As day by day crept on life's cares;
And still my ship is out at sea—
Perchance she may yet return to me.

*   *   *   *   *   *

There is a shore beyond the grave,
Where the troubled waters cease to rave,
Where the halcyon calm of holy peace,
Through endless ages will not cease
To shed its radiance o'er the few,
Who, to the last, are staunch and true,
Here, in the welkin, moon and stars,
Planets and meteors drive their cars;

Here, too, the sun gives warmth and light,—
But all commingled are not as bright
As the shining mansions where the blest
After life's fitful fever rest.
Here our frail barks may not come back,
Or leave a trace of their onward track
To point out the hidden mystery
Of ships that have gone down at sea.

———

LIFE'S HOLIDAY.

Children at play !
How joyous, how happy and careless are they:
Chasing the butterflies over the lea,
Culling the blossoms from every tree,
Gathering the daisies and buttercups gay,
Making the most of their brief holiday.
Theirs is the present, unclouded and bright ;
Theirs is the future, resplendent with light ;
Life's merry morning is fleeting away—
Learn ye a lesson from children at play.

Careless and free !
Is youth in its noontide of glad revelry :
The present is tinged with a roseate hue,
With friends ever constant, loves tender and true :
The world not too wide a domain for their sway,
Hope smiling aloof, Faith guiding their way;
Onward, still onward, some object in view,
Some bright changeful meteor still to pursue,
Till the rainbow hues vanish from life's iron chain,
And only the memories of pleasure remain.

Care sets its signet on manhood's calm brow,
Long ere the crisp locks are frosted with snow—
The step may be light and the smile still be gay,
But life's rosiest visions are fleeting away,
Leaving a shadow their steps to attend,
In the absence of wealth or the loss of a friend.
Let pride erect castles for others to gain,
Let the jovial still echo the song of the vain,
Let the miser win gold, let the hero gain fame,
Give the lover his idol, the poet a name—
Every heart hath its secret of shadow and gloom
As it journeys along on its way to the tomb.

THE BELLS.

The bells are gaily ringing,
   And on the summer gale,
Their notes of joy are bringing,
   An oft-told tale !
Two lovers now are kneeling
   At hymen's shrine,
And midst their joyful pealing,
   Fond hearts entwine !

Again their sounds are dying
   Upon the blast,
The dead is coldly lying,
   A soul hath past:
Where droops the graceful willow,
   They laid him low,
The cold earth for his pillow,
   With tears of woe.

The bells are wildly clashing,
   A field is won :
There have been sabres flashing
   In the summer sun ;
We hear the widows' sighing,
   For the mighty slain,
We see the dead and dying,
   In one heap lain.

4*

Again the sounds are stealing
   Upon the ear,
And to the heart revealing,
   The hour of prayer ;
And at the altar lowly,
   The humble kneel,
Upon the breeze rides slowly,
   A holy peal.

We see the pilgrims kneeling,
   In holy prayer,
When convent bells are stealing
   Upon the ear ;
At morn, mid-day, and even,
   In Mary's praise,
And souls communed with Heaven,
   In other days !

MAY-DAY IN THE OLDEN TIME.

A hundred years ago,
   And a hundred years before,
When the smiling month of May
   Strewed her sweets on mead and moor ;

When the hawthorn in the shade,
　With its blossoms fresh and gay,
Was the wreath each rustic maid
　Wore in honor of the day :
When the May-pole on the lawn,
　Where the "lads and lassies" met,
To dance from early dawn,
　Till the sun at eve had set,
Was festooned around with garlands, fresh and
　　green ;
　Oh! these were merry days,
　And we love the rural lays,
Sung in honor of the charming May-day Queen!

A hundred years ago,
　And a hundred years before,
When the dew-drops glistened on each leaf and
　　flower ;
　Our grandmamas arose,
　Ere the sun begun his course,　　　.
To wash their faces with the bright and pearly
　　shower ;
　Like Diana, each one strove
　Their beauty to improve,
And to keep their roseate blushes soft and bright,
　So before the dawn of day,
　To the meads they took their way,
Ere the sun dispelled the shadows of the night ;

We watch them as they pass,
  Tripping lightly o'er the grass,
And listen to their laughter, light and gay,
  As we see the pearly shower
  Shaken from the opening flower,
At the dawning of the beautiful May-day!

These are day-dreams of the past,
  That no sky can overcast,
And the present by comparison is pale,
  As its toils and trials sweep
  Through the visions of our sleep,
As trying as an "oft told tale!"
  Oh! the days of long ago
  Held no semblance of woe,
Life's rosy hours, no record of despair,
  Now we loiter on the way,
  And the blooming month of May,
Only from our days, cuts off another year:
  No more, on lawn or green,
  Is crowned a rustic queen,
No more the May-pole's wreathed with garlands gay,
  No more at early dawn,
  The dew-drops from the thorn,
Are shaken from the fragrant scented May!

We are old and wiser grown,
Our youthful tares are sown,
And the harvest of our deeds we reap with pain,
   To escape eternal loss,
   We must humbly bear the cross,
Hoping happiness hereafter to attain.

THE EXILED ARAB'S SONG.

Oh, for a home in the desert wild,
   When summer days are fair,
For a bounding steed and faithful dog
   My free campaign to share.
The one should bear me to the chase,
   The other track my prey,
And both should share my resting-place
   At the close of the glorious day.

By night I dream of the boundless plains,
   Of my distant fatherland,
And by day I sigh to join again
   My old familiar band;
To scour—to almost skim—the ground
   On my own fleet-footed steed,
Or wake the slumbering echoes round,
   As of old, with my tuneful reed.

I long to slake my thirst once more
    At the springs of the desert wild,
To brave the heat, as in days of yore,
    As becomes an Arab child.
What to me is the wine so red and bright
    That dyes the social cup,
Compared with a draught in a hasty flight,
    When my own hand raised it up?

My free-born limbs refuse to move
    Along the crowded street,
Though long ago I was wont to rove,
    (The whirlwind scarce less fleet.)
I find no joys on this foreign ground
    To compare with a wandering life,
Where my resting-place on the earth I found
    When tired with the chase or strife.

What warrior would leave his spear in rest
    To rust on a painted wall;
Would don his limbs in a silken vest
    And his steed leave in its stall?
Both man and horse would soon forget
    Their freedom in such place,
And sunk in sloth would cease to regret
    The joys of the bounding chase.

SING NOT THAT SONG TO-NIGHT.

Oh! not to-night, sing not to-night
    That sweet and touching strain;
Those sounds that once gave me delight
    Now fill my heart with pain.
When last those cheerful words were sung,
    Her voice joined in the lay,
Now uttered by a stranger's tongue,
    None seem so sad as they.
That broken lute hath lost a string—
    Oh! leave it to repose;
Those few sweet words, oh! do not sing
    Before the heart's wound close.

They tell me time will soon efface
    The memory of the past,
And soon again the coldness chase,
    Now o'er my senses cast.
It may be so—but this I know,
    The Present hath no power,
To break the icy chill of woe
    Cast o'er me in that hour.
Though she hath passed to brighter spheres,
    To regions of delight,
I cannot listen without tears,—
    Sing not that song to-night.

A MORNING IN MAY.

Oh ! 'tis joyful to rise in the morning,
   And welcome the sun's early rays,
As their radiance the landscape adorning,
   Sing carols of Infinite praise.
Hear the choir of the linnets and thrushes,
   The robin's soft language of love,
The twittering wrens in the bushes,
   The merry lark warbling above.

How sweetly the breezes are sighing,
   As they play with the opening leaves,
The rippling of waters replying,
   Forgetting the winter's cold graves,
Where the myriad insects are sleeping,
   That sang to the last year's gay flowers ;
Where the evergreen ivy was creeping
   Around these cool arbors of ours.

To give " care to the winds " for a season,
   Is philosophy, sages will say;
Let it never be reckoned a treason
   To rejoice in the sweet month of May.
Come forth to the country, ye weary !
   Here, here is enjoyment for all ;
The sunshine will make your hearts cheery,
   Kind nature will welcome your call.

The earth is adorned like a maiden,
　Whose gems are the sweet-scented May,
The wealth of whose tresses are laden
　With garlands as bright as the day.
The buds of the apple and cherry
　Are bursting to life on the trees ;
The chirping grasshopper is merry,
　And busy the emmets and bees.

The daisies are dimpling the meadows,
　The violets are hid in the wood,
The daffodil flaunts in the shadows,
　Where the trees have for centuries stood ;
Every weed hath its use and its mission,
　Every atom its little life's span,—
But whatever the change or transition
　All Nature is subject to Man.

———

THE RIVALS.

Lady Ellen has gems of the costliest kind,
　Sparkling diamonds and rubies bright ;
I have only—my hair to bind—
　The flowerets wet with the dews of night.
Lady Ellen's hands are white as milk,
　And her golden tresses hang loosely down,
Over shimmering robes of the softest silk ;
　My dress is plain, and my hands are brown.

Lady Ellen's voice is like a bird,
  With thrilling cadence soft and low,
And when she sings, you would think you heard
  The murmuring winds dissolving the snow.
I warble, because my heart is light,
  Wholly untutored, wild and free,
My ebon hair is like shades of night,
  And when unconfined, reaches down to my knee.

There is one whom both would wish to win,
  Of noble birth and high degree ;
He dwells, the castle's walls within,
  And often wanders forth with me.
He calls me his beautiful nut-brown maid,
  And praises my curls of raven hair,
And whispers, soon 'neath the woodland shade,
  His honored name I shall proudly bear.

I am lowly born, but I fear no frown,
  My heart is light and my face is fair,
Like the chestnut burrs, are my eyes dark brown,
  And soft as silk is my raven hair.
He is my captive and willing slave,
  And if I ever become his bride,
The frowns of this world he will have to bear,
  But then, I will humbly veil my pride.

"I MISS THEE FROM MY SIDE."

I miss thee from my side
   At the cheerful dawn of day,
As by the pebbly shore
   I take my lonely way;
When I gaze upon the deep, deep sea,
   And listen to its roar,
I sigh to hear thy gentle voice
   As heard in days of yore.

I miss thy kindly smile,
   When my heart is full of glee ;
I miss thy sweet companionship,
   Thy soothing sympathy;
I lack thy gentle chiding
   To curb the rising pride,
That sometimes steals around my heart,—
   I miss thee from my side.

I miss thee when the song of birds
   Makes woodland echoes ring ;
When the modest daisy on the plain
   Proclaims the coming spring ;
When the white May casts its spangles
   Upon the lowly thorn,
And we were wont to wander forth
   At eve and dewy morn.

As I gaze upon the landscape—
    Hill, dale and flowery lea,
The mountain heights, the beetling rocks,
    The vast and boundless sea;
I fancy that I hear thy voice
    In answer to my own;
'Tis then I miss thee from my side,
    'Tis then I feel alone.

I love to muse on pleasures gone,—
    The memories of the past,
Too surely prove that human ties
    Are far too frail to last;
The sunlight on the dancing wave
    The lightest cloud can veil,
So the lorn heart, from human ken,
    Its sorrows can conceal.

This world is all too cold and stern
    To break the secret spell,
That ivy-like confines the heart
    Within its mystic cell;
True friendship only hath the power
    To read what we would hide,
To share our joys, to soothe our woes,—
    "I miss thee from my side."

JUNE.

The mysterious voices of nature
   Are whispering from day unto day,
The birds of the woods are the heralds,
   The flowers, the handmaidens gay;
The sunbeams that spangle the waters,
   The zephyrs that sport with the leaves,
The emmets that toil all the summer,
   The green grass that covers the graves.

Kind Nature hath summoned her children,
   And the roses of June are in bloom ;
Some will smile on our festival hours,
   Others brighten the funeral gloom ;
Youthful beauty and flowers are well mated,
   And the sombre graves cold earthly bands
Lose the shade that would otherwise veil them
   By flowers from friends loving hands.

On the plains the young lambkins are sporting,
   The lark shakes the dew from its wings,
As ascending from earth towards Heaven
   The air with its melody rings ;

The bees are collecting their treasures,
　　The grasshopper chirps all the day,
The woodpecker taps at the elm-tree,
　　All nature is happy and gay.

The merchant shuts day-book and ledger,
　　The school-boy from bondage is free,
The artist leaves palette and easel
　　And wends to the mountains or sea.
The poet awakes from his dreaming,
　　The beauty leaves revel and ball,
All respond to the magical voices
　　With which Nature her votaries call.

———

THE BRIDE.

With pearls they bound her raven hair,
　　Upon her bridal day,
And in a robe of spotless white
　　Did her fair form array;
They bid her check the rising sigh,
　　And dry the falling tear,
That shone upon her damask cheek
　　Like the pearls within her hair.

The pale white orange blossom,
    And snowy veil are worn,
To grace and shade a maiden fair
    Upon her bridal morn :
But tears will often dim the eye,
    Even when hearts are given
To those who are the chosen ones,
    Destined to wed by Heaven.

Such tears are dry as soon as shed,
    And beaming smiles repay
The one that swears to cherish
    And guard with love the way,
The blended path for good or ill,
    That both may have to share,   •
For which the maiden leaves her home
    And parents' tender care.

Well may this peerless maiden weep
    In memory of the past,
When called upon to sacrifice
    He first love and her last ;
To break the vows of mutual troth
    That bound their hearts in one,
And give her hand to one who hath
    No charm save gold alone.

Can wealth give back sweet peace of mind,
  Or dry up beauty's tear,
Or save the young and tender heart
  From hastening to its bier?
If so, go spread the nuptial feast,
  Call all to share your pride,
Exult that you have won your child
  By fraud to be a bride.

Heed not her pale and quivering lip,
  Or the tear-drop gathering fast;
Give " gold " to soothe and solace her
  For the joys that now are past.
And even when her parting breath
  Calls on another's name,
Ask not your heart whose was the fault,
  Ask not whose was the blame?

Save your own hearts, if hearts you have,
  From unavailing pain;
Break the gold circle, loose the bond,
  And bid her smile again;
The flowers are fair that bind her brow,
  The pearls their radiance cast,
The present hath no charms for her—
  Her thoughts are with the past.

Gold is a glittering evil,
  The bane of sordid age—
A bond that may control the will,
  Though not the heart engage;
It cannot bind a broken heart
  Or teach it to forget;
Affection is the only balm
  To shield us from regret.

———

THE DRUNKARD'S HOME.

The wild winds shook the feeble door,
  Where a shivering baby slept,
Cold was the room, and damp the floor,
  Where its youthful mother wept;
A single taper glimmered there,
  Whose light in that dreary place
Was shed on a face, like moonlight fair,
  And form of touching grace.

5

She sat by a fireless grate alone,
　　With no one to soothe her fears,
The joyous light of her eye was gone,
　　Her pale cheek, wet with tears !
She thought of her home 'neath cloudless skies,
　　Of its sunset bright and warm,
And she wept o'er the shivering babe that lies
　　Asleep 'midst the gathering storm.

She listened for one, whose varied lot
　　She had vowed through life to share,
Her breath she hushed, but he cometh not,
　　She hath raised her voice in prayer,
That once again his step might bless,
　　And his voice some kindness own,
And she sighed in very tenderness,
　　As she thought of that reckless one !

He sat where the circling glass was shared,
　　With the warm fire's spreading glow,
Where the merry song and jest were heard,
　　Nor thought of that mourner's woe ;
Forgot, is the wife who was once so dear,
　　The babe, he was wont to caress,　　　　.
And *reason* is drowned in the drunkard's cheer,
　　And *love* in the harlot's kiss.

THE MUSIC OF THE NIGHT WIND.

When the stars are seen in the cloudless sky
    I would wander forth with thee,
And list to the mighty minstrelsy,
    Of the wild wind wandering free,
As it plays with the giant things of earth,
    Unseen by mortal eyes,
To all unknown, its wondrous birth,
    Or the founts from which it rise.

It tosses the waves of the boundless sea,
    And shivers the tapering mast ;
It sighs midst the leaves of the forest tree,
    Like memories of the past ;
It trembles amidst the garden blooms,
    As it sweeps like a spirit by,
And where the cypress weeps o'er the tombs,
    It answers, sigh for sigh.

When the pearls of Heaven hang on the thorn,
    And silence reigns around,
It comes with the earliest blush of morn,
    With a gentle murmuring sound ;
It rides o'er the fields, when the harvest-moon
    Looks down on the golden grain,
And sings with a gay and joyous tone,
    As it dashes over the plain.

THE LOVELINESS OF NATURE.

I love the sky, the vaulted sky,
   When the silver moon illumes the night;
I love the host of golden stars
   That there unfold their dreamy light.
The sun that plows the bright domain,
   The summer fleecy clouds that lie
Like heaps of snow in azure blue,—
   I love the sky! I love the sky!

I love the snowdrops that unfold
   Their snowy vests in earliest spring,
And crocus, with their hues of gold,
   That to the mind bright promise bring;
The modest daisy on the lea,
   The violet in the shady grove,
The lily bell, the scented pea,
   All blossoms of this earth I love.

The beauty of the boundless main,
   The music of the sounding shore,
The rocks that breast the swelling tide,
   The crested foam, the ocean's roar;
The meanest pebble on the beach,
   The seaweed green, the sounding shell,
The spray, the breeze, the music wild,
   The sea bird's cry,—I love them well!

I love the earth, its rocks and glens,
  Its fertile fields and slumbering vales,
The forest tree and flowery shrub,
  The plains, the hills, the sunny dales ;
I love the early blush of morn,
  The twilight with its shadows gray,
The dancing sunbeams on the rills,
  All have their charms,—I love the day !

The tempest in the clouded sky,
  The thunder's voice, the whirlwind drear,
The rush of waters, song of birds,
  The whistling winds I love to hear ;
The snow that falls in fleecy clouds
  And clothes creation like a pall,
The soft, refreshing summer showers,—
  I love them all ! I love them all !

The sea; the earth, the wond'rous whole ;
  The stars, the waves, the flowerets bright ;
The winds, the clouds, the murmuring rills,
  All fill my soul with keen delight.
But most I love the kindred soul,
  The constant friend, so often proved,
Who soothes my woes and shares my joys,
  And proves his right to be beloved.

THE WIND.

A song for the wild, wild breeze,
  The chainless and the free,
That sings 'midst forest trees
  And rusheth o'er the sea.
It hath bent the hazel bough,
  Where hangs the wild bird's nest,
Swept o'er the spotless snow
  That clothed the mountain breast.
Rifled the garden blooms
  At the earliest blush of morn,
Hath passed o'er fertile fields
  And bent the ripening corn.

A song for the rushing wind
  That hath no resting-place—
It wanders unconfined
  O'er all creation's face.
It is heard in the genial spring,
  As it chides the frost away,
And welcome tidings bring,
  Of seasons still more gay;
When summer suns are bright,
  And the trees are robed with green,
We hail it with delight
  Amidst each sylvan scene.

It fills the fluttering sails
   Of the vessel on the deep,
And speaks of distant vales
   To the sailor in his sleep ;
He listens to its roar,
   And again in fancy stands
Beside his cottage door,
   In far-off distant lands.
Where the sick man bows his head,
   Again its restless wings,
If fluttering round his bed
   A sweet refreshment brings.

A song to the mighty wind,
   Of strange, mysterious birth—
No human art can bind
   It to our mother earth.
It stirs the humblest flower
   That decks the cottage door,
Plays with the summer-shower,
   And in the tempest's roar
Shivers the forest tree,
   And rives the gallant mast,
And e'en the mighty sea
   Will howl beneath its blast.

"USE, AND NOT ABUSE."

Time is swiftly flying,
    Let us spend it well,
Every new-born hour
    Rings the last one's knell ;
Passed away forever,
    On its heavenward track,
All the wealth of nations
    Cannot win it back.
In the mystic balance
    Of eternity,
All our words and actions,
    Thoughts and wishes lie ;
Here, our will is potent,
    Good or ill to choose,
Then let our maxim be,
    " To use, and not abuse."

We are Heaven's stewards
    In our little day,
Talents to us given
    To gild our onward way;
To feed the poor and needy
    Should be the rich man's care,
The strong to help the weak,
    The gay the sad to cheer.

With love to bear the trials
  God in his wisdom sends,
Kind thoughts for all our foes,
  Kind words for all our friends ;
Every fleeting moment
  We good or ill may choose,
Then let our maxim be,
  "To use, and not abuse."

Wealth, and peace, and plenty
  Lent us for a span,
Health, and strength, and beauty,
  Heaven's best gifts to man ;
Household ties and treasures,
  Chains that bind the heart,
When our love is strongest,
  One by one depart.
Waste no time in mourning,
  Shed no useless tears,
Hope will soothe the trials
  Of succeeding years ;
Life hath still its blessings,
  Nothing good refuse,
But let our maxim be,
  "To use, and not abuse."

5*

HOME.

It is home where the heart is,
  In mansion or cot,
Sanctified by affection;
  No home,—where 'tis not;
Where true hearts assemble,
  And kind voices blend;
Where smiles greet the advent
  Of wife, husband or friend.

It is home where the heart is,
  Untrammeled by care,
Misfortune may enter,
  It remaineth not there;
As a cloud o'er a fountain
  Obscureth the light,
Till the glow of the sunbeam
  Again lends its light.

It is home where the heart is,
  Though lowly the door,
The walls may be naked,
  Uncovered the floor;
The fare may be frugal,
  The habiliments plain,
Peace and love may abide there,
  Dispelling the pain.

It is home where the heart is
    Unchilled by disdain,
Where love binds the flowers,
    On life's rugged chain ;
Where the ills of the present,
    Its crosses and cares,
'Neath the smiles of affection
    Like the mist disappears.

THE CITY OF THE DEAD.

The morning sun with cheerful rays,
    Looks down on the graves of the silent dead,
On the lettered stones, whose words of praise
    Preserve their memory undecayed.

The flowers planted by loving hands,
    The funeral garlands wet with tears,
Column or sculptured pillar stands,
    Beside the emblem Faith reveres.

Here we see where a father sleeps,
    Where a tender mother is laid to rest,
And the summer flower the record keeps,
    Of an infant clasped to its mother's breast.

Sisters—pure as the angels are,
  Brothers—the bravest earth has seen,
Partners in life, faithful and fair,
  Sleep under the sod of emerald green.

Silent and lone is their resting place,
  Though lovingly tended with pious care,
It will lead the soul to the Throne of Grace,
  And raise in the heart a silent prayer.

Every tree that bends above,
  Every flower in its bloom and fall,
Mournfully calls for some act of love,
  In this City of Death from one and all.

JULY.

The grass is newly mown,
And ready hands have strewn
The fragrant burthen to the scorching July sun ;
From the scattered faded swathe,
The rick is deftly made,
And the farmer looks with joy and pride thereon.

The kine stand in the shade,
Or in the brooklet wade,
The sheep are of their snowy fleece relieved ;
List,—to the bleating lambs,
And the answering of their dams,
As their liberty again each hath received.

July hath fruits and flowers,
Cool grots, and leafy bowers,
And with bounteous hand her blessings she bestows ;
See the lily on the stream,
Its waxen flowers gleam,
Pure as the wreathes of winter's driven snows.

Now, 'tis pleasant to recline
Where the leafy branches twine,
And to watch the crystal waters as they flow;
To escape from toil and heat,
And in some cool retreat,
Enjoy the luxury that leisure can bestow.

HATRED.

Who can bid the human soul
The baleful seeds of hate control?
If once its germ finds entrance there,
It feeds on all things good and fair;
Then serpent-like its track is seen,
Where kindly thoughts have fostered been;
No gentle virtue can have place,
Where hate presents its odious face.

Peace dwells not in the troubled breast;
Her gentle wing would find no rest
Where hate keeps guard to bar her way;
She could not brook its tyrant sway—
Where thoughts of vengeance seem to sleep,
Yet only strike their roots more deep,
Like murderer, waiting for his foe,
Seeking to aim the deadly blow.

The heart that worships at its shrine
Clothes every object with its slime,
As coil by coil its links are wove,
Where once dwelt faith, and peace, and love.
Who dares to breathe the simple word,
That in our daily prayers is heard :
" Forgive"—as I my brother spare—
While hate is only cherished there !

Ah ! who would forfeit peace of mind,
A moment's base revenge to find—
The open brow with blushes stain,
To cause a fellow-creature pain :
Such base revenge no joy could bring,
But only cause sins deadliest sting
To rankle in the tortured heart—
Beware of hate whoe'er thou art !

AN INVITATION TO THE COUNTRY.

Come forth to the country,
    From city and town,
Leave the web on the loom,
    Cast your handiwork down ;
Come forth while the dog-roses
    Hang on the spray,
Ere the warblers are mute,
    At the close of the day !

Come forth to the woods,
  Where the blackberries grow,
To the meads, where the rippling brooks
  Carelessly flow.
Oh! 'tis pleasant to rest
  'Neath the wide-spreading trees,
In fields, where the ripening corn
  Bends to the breeze.

The soft airs of summer
  Have caught from the earth,
The various perfumes
  That from her have their birth;
On the hedges the woodbine,
  Its sweet flowers hath hung,
And beside them the wreathes
  Of the bind-weed are flung;
By the rivers, the bulrush,
  Hath lifted its head,
And the butter-cups' bells
  O'er the meadows are spread—
Come forth! oh, come forth!
  Here are pleasures for all;
For the young and the old,
  For the great and the small.

Come forth to the country,
  Thou maiden so fair,
And cull the wild flow'ret
  To braid with thy hair;
Dost thou love? Ah! that sigh
  Tells a tale of its own!

Come forth, oh ! thou fair one,
   But come not alone.
For but little thou'lt heed
   If alone thou dost stray,
The flowers of the field,
   The wild birds on the spray.
But, if in sweet converse,
   These pleasures are shared,
To thy heart, all that's bright,
   Will be doubly endeared.

Old man ! dost thou seek
   The calm blessing to share,
That springs from content,
   From retirement, and prayer ?
Here are shrines—here are altars—
   Come bow ye at them.
Every leaf hath its song,
   Every blade hath its hymn !
On the hills the bright sunbeams
   Are tinging with brown,
The sweet-scented heather,
   On which he looks down ;
And the grasshopper's song,
   And the busy bees' hum,
All join in one call—
   And invite thee to come !

Come forth ! thou young student,
  And bask in its beams,
Leave thy lamp and thy tomes,
  And thy various dreams ;
Try the scenes of the country,
  Its gentle repose,
Will call back to thy pale cheek,
  The hues of the rose !
And you who are busy
  Increasing your store—
Come, rest for a while,
  And the hard task give o'er !
Seek health in the country,
  On mountain and plain,
For without this best blessing
  All else will be vain !

"A THING OF BEAUTY IS A JOY FOR EVER."

Do I love beauty ?   Yes,
  My heart can dearly feel
The charms of loveliness
  Around its senses steal !
And I love Nature's face,
  Because that face is fair ;
God's goodness I can trace
  In the beauties lavished there.

The lily of the vale,
  (Like vestal clothed in white)
Whose scent rides on the gale,
  Before it glads our sight,
And the modest violet blue,
  That blooms on rugged ground,
Full dearly prized are you,
  Where'er your flowers are found.

The wild-rose on the spray,
  That bends with every gale,
And e'en the gems of May,
  With lightsome heart I hail!
God gave the perfume sweet
  To every little flower,
And cast them at our feet,
  That we might bless his power.

When winter chills the air,
  And brighter blooms are dead,
The little snow-drop fair
  Uprears its pearly head;
And in the garden bed
  The yellow crocus gleams,
And primrose lifts its head,
  To hail day's early beams.

The stately forest tree
  Adorns the woodland shade,
Where in perfect liberty
  The wild-birds' nest is made;
And on its topmost spray
  The cawing rooks appear,
Building at break of day
  In the spring-time of the year.

Upon the verdant hills
  The wild thyme lures the bee,
Its humble hive it fills
  With the sweets from hill and lea;
I joy to hear the sound
  Of its tiny bugle near,
As it flutters o'er the ground
  When summer suns appear.

There is Beauty everywhere,
  On hill, in dale, and grove,
And all that's sweet and fair
  My heart can dearly love,
From the floweret on the thorn,
  To the blue and changeful sky,
The wild bees' hum at morn,
  To the merry lark's reply.

THE ANGEL OF LIFE.

When first from the chaos that hung o'er the earth,
  The Eternal commanded the light to appear,
When the garden of Eden amidst the bright birth
  Of Creation shone brightest—and Man was placed
    there—
When the songs of the spirits of light, breathed
    around
  The same airs that were hymned near the Crea-
    tor's Throne,
And the freshness of life had adorned the bright
    ground,
  Man sighed, as he thought he must live there
    alone.

Though bright were the fountains, and pleasant the
    bowers,
  And new glories sprung up as the swift moments
    · flew,
And sweet was the fragrance that breathed from the
    flowers,
  And all things shone forth, as with Heaven's own
    hue,
Still Man 'midst creation was pensive and sad,
  A something he sought to make dearly his own,
A something to make even Eden more glad,—
  Woman came, and his heart felt no longer alone.

The seraphs pressed round at her mystical birth,
  The last and best gift of creation to guard;
With her grace and her beauty, she came to this
      earth,—
  And to this day remains,—still the dearest reward
That man can be blest with,—for who hath not seen
  The hearts that beat wildest for fame and renown,
Consider those laurels more deathless and green,
  That are wreathed by the hands of dear woman
      alone?

In sunshine or sorrow, in sickness or health,
  'Midst the crowds of the city, or lonely fireside,
Should the cold blasts of poverty scatter our wealth,
  And our hearts feel the withering meanness of
      pride;
When adversity enters, though cold is its frown,
  The light as a beacon still gleams o'er our path,
The deeper the anguish, the clearer 'tis shown !
  And this boon that is left to illumine the earth,
Is the influence of woman, and her love alone.

When life hath its moments of radiant delight,
  And ambition hath taught the young spirit to soar,
When hope hovers round us and all appears bright,
  As safe from the tempest we anchor on shore;

When the clouds that pass o'er us but serve to en-
    dear
The gems that we gather, or flowers that we twine,
The fairest possession, when all things look fair,
    Are the smiles that make happiness still more
    divine.

And who when the sorrows of life press the heart,
    Or sickness hath set its sad seal on the brow,
Would wish from this Angel of Life to depart,
    Or refuse the sweet influence love can bestow?
From our birth, like a spell, is her magical sway,
    As in childhood we turn from a world yet un-
    known,
And till death, half the sunshine that cheers our
    sad way,
    Is the influence of woman and her love alone.

Then who would refuse to acknowledge the spell,
    That sorrow can lighten, and joy can impart;
Who against the bright influence e'er would rebel,
    That woman can weave round the sensitive heart?
This world were a wilderness, lonely and sad,
    And joyless on Earth had our pilgrimage been,
Even Adam in Eden—refused to be glad,
    Till the beauty of Woman, illumined the scene.

SONG.

Oh, Dennis, my darling !
Give over your snarling,
And come down with me
    To the sycamore tree ;
For musical Paddy,
This hour has been ready,
And the boys and the girls
    Are dancing with glee.

Sure mirth is no treason,
And youth is the season,
When light hearts and light feet
    Take their fullness of joy;
Why are you so jealous
Of all the young fellows,
Whilst at Fair, and at Wake,
    You're a broth of a boy ?

When you danced with young Mary,
Down at Castle-Gary,
Did I pout and look cross,
    As you oft do with me ?
If you do not be " aisy,"
You will drive me quite crazy.
And I shall run off, sir,
    Across the big " say !"

This useless delaying,
Whilst the music is playing,
Will *sure* make dissension,
   Betwixt you and me,
Then, Dennis, my darling !
Give over your snarling,
Your Kathleen's as constant,
   As constant can be.

CASTLES IN THE AIR.

Build ye castles stout and strong,
  With lofty towers and stately spires,
Adorn the halls with taste and skill,
  And gratify your hearts' desires ;
Let rippling waters ebb and flow,
  And gardens blossom fresh and fair,
But if these only *wishes* are—
  They are but " Castles in the Air."

Count your friends by tens of score,
  Seat them round your generous board,
Let it groan with dainties rare,
  Reckon no gold you wish to hoard ;
6

Let music lend its gentle charm,
    Bid pain and sorrow disappear,
But if these only *wishes* are,—
    They are but " Castles in the Air."

Assist the struggling poor to live,
    And cheer the heart with grief opprest;
Speak words of counsel, faith and hope,
    To soothe the sufferer's aching breast;
Visit the sick and bury the dead,
    O'er human woes drop pity's tear,
But if these only *wishes* are,—
    They are but " Castles in the Air."

Should these our stately castles fall,
    And summer friends look coldly on,
Should pain or sorrow chill the soul,
    With no true heart to lean upon;
Let us no useless record keep,
    Of what perchance we might have been,
Had those bright fancies of our youth
    Still kept faith's garlands fresh and green.

AUGUST.

Now cometh brown August with sickle in hand,
To collect the rich stores from the bountiful land,
The dew on her buskin, the rose on her cheeks,
And the wild merry laugh, that a light heart be-
    speaks ;
She calls on the rustic to share in her glee,
For the harvest is gathered on upland and lea,
The apples are garnered, both rosy and brown,
Secure from the frost-king, with care fastened down.

The swallows have vanished, the reed-birds appear,
From the fair sunny South, our marshes to cheer ;
The lone whip-poor-will from its own leafy bower,
With its spirit like wailing, is counting each hour ;
The wonderful mocking bird hides in the shade,
From morning till eve in the forest arcade,
Where he imitates every note that is heard,
And seems to be more like a fay than a bird.

Now myriads of fire-flies enliven the scene,
With their golden sparks glistening the dark trees
    between ;
The bat flaps his wings, as he circles around,
Now aloof, and now seeming to dip on the ground ;
The shriek of the owl, the fierce hiss of the snake,
And the plash of the waters, the echoes awake ;
The drone of the bullfrog, the katydid's call,
Are the sounds of the season familiar to all.

AN INQUIRY.

I asked of the sparkling dew-drops,
    That hung on the opening flowers,
"If anything fairer had passed that way,
As they had kept watch since the break of day,
    Counting the minutes and hours ?"
The blushing rose and lily pale
    Had been kissed by the wandering bee ;
So tossing the pearls from each glowing leaf,
    And, smiling, they answered me :
"The fairest gem 'neath the sun-lit sky
    Is a maiden adorned with purity !"

I questioned the stars in the midnight sky,
Shining like diamonds on mountain and plain,
To tell me the name of the fairest gem
In the silent night that looked up to them ;
And soft and low the whisper came,
And still again was heard the name
Of the being, the rose and lily express'd
As the brightest, purest, best ;
"The fairest pearl 'neath a star-lit sky
Is a maiden of spotless purity !"

I called aloud to the summer gale,
   That played with my hair and fanned my cheek,
And bid it rest on its rapid wing,
As it rifled the sweets from the blossoms of spring,
Whilst the air was faint with the odors of flowers
That faded and died in the woodland bowers
   Unseen by mortal eyes ;
Again the answer came, breathing to me
   The same as the one from the stars and flowers :
"The fairest thing on earth or sea
Is a maiden adorned with purity !"

The best and fairest form on earth,
   The brightest pearl old ocean bears,
The compeer of the sweetest flower,
   The gem that hearth and home endears ;

The kindest friend, when friends are kind,
 Who makes this earth a Paradise,
Whose chains the fiercest foe can bind,
 And bid the drooping spirit rise:
Even the monarch of the plains,
 The lordly lion, turns and flies,
From the all-conquering magic glance,
 That emanate from woman's eyes.

———

PASSING AWAY.

The glories of summer are passing away,
Already its roses begin to decay;
The leaves on the trees have a lighter green,
And a change appears in each sylvan scene;
The morning sun later awakens the rills,
And the mist rests longer upon the hills;
The wind hath a sadder and deeper sound,
As if its mighty wings were bound;
And it pined for the blossoms that were so gay
But whose glories, from earth, are *Passing Away!*

We missed not the gentle departure of Spring,
For the birds were aloof on dewy wing,
And their music was heard so wild and gay,
As they hailed the glorious God of day;
The wreathes of May, and the violets blue,
Looked brighter when decked with the drops of dew;
The apple, and cherry, put forth their leaves,
And the swallow was building beneath the eaves,
All Nature was looking so fresh and fair,
That we missed not the first-born of the year.

But Summer, sweet Summer, when thou shalt flee,
The blossoms, and flowers, will vanish with thee ;
Then, bounteous Autumn shall reign for awhile,
Till tyrant Winter shall blight thy smile.
Just such is life.   In our childhood's hours
We heed not the thorns as we cull the flowers,
All, then is sunlight, and golden dreams,
And only the Future more beauteous seems,
Where pleasure, ambition, and love, hold their
    sway,
Till we find, one by one, they are *Passing Away.*

LONELINESS.

Alone! who hath not felt alone?
  Even when this world's smiles were given;
Who hath not felt his spirit's tone,
  Sink like a falling star at even!
Who ever deemed the prize when won
  Worth half the labor it had cost?
Alone! who hath not felt alone,
  Even when prized and worshipped most?

Take the first morning of life's day,
  When all things wore their brightest hue,
And looked as fair as vernal May,
  And were as frail and shadowy too.
Call back as with a wizard's wand
  The forms that fluttered o'er our path,
And made the world a fairy land,
  With scarce a stain or shade of earth.

And, if the retrospection brings
  Those cherished beings still as bright,
As when our first imaginings
  Clothed all things with their own sweet light;
Then hath the heart one lovely beam
  To blend amidst life's future day—
One memory, bright as love's first dream,
  To cheer our solitary way.

Alone! Who hath not turned aside,
   When joy was heard and mirth was loud,
Their tears of bitterness to hide,
   And felt alone amidst the crowd?
A look, or tone had power to bring
   Some treasured memory to the mind,
Like the sweet harp whose viewless string
   Is sighed upon by every wind.

Who hath not smiled with breaking heart,
   And felt the chill and throb of woe;
Yet proudly tore those links apart
   That caused such maddening tears to flow?
And turned with glance of pride away,
   Lest the soul's anguish should be shown
By the pale lip and moistened eye,
   And felt that they were all alone?

This loneliness of soul will show
   That earth is not our resting-place;
As human friendships work us woe,
   And we sin's serpent track can trace.
Then let us still the troubled heart
   With calm religion's holy tone,
And tear those earthly chains apart
   That·bind us to this world alone.

6*

THE HEATHER-BELL OF SCOTLAND.

The rose is bright in my lady's bower,
　　Where the jasmine trails its wreath,
The rich parterre hath many a flower,
　　But my choice is the purple heath !
It gleams where the tawny gypsy rests,
　　Where the truant school-boys roam,
Seeking to rob the "birdies" nests,
　　That lie hid in the "bonnie broom."

Tho' lowly its stem, the wandering bee
　　Delights in its tiny bells,
Whose incense ascends from the grassy lea;
　　With the wind from its secret cells ;
It needs no culture, but fresh and green
　　Springs up from the barren earth,
Where human footsteps have rarely been,
　　Its waxen bells have birth.

It is seen where the red deer nimbly bounds,
　　Where the heath-cock lifts its head, ·
And seeketh to save from the baying hounds
　　The hare in its fragrant bed.
Then hail to the plant of the hardy North,
　　To the gem of the mountain and lea,
Fit emblem it seemeth of modest worth,
　　Oh, the bonnie heath-bell for me.

THE REVEL OF THE FAY.

The dog-rose is closed on its tremulous spray,
And the songsters are silent, "Arise, sister Fay,
We will dance in the moonbeams that gleam on the
    ground,
And sing to the night breeze that flutters around,
And then to the couch of the maiden we'll fly
Who shall dream the light step of her lover is nigh,
That she kneels at the altar, and over her brow
The folds of the nuptial veil carelessly flow."

" And then by the slumbering miser we'll stand,
And tease him with gold that escapes from his hand,
Dance over his temples, and laugh at the pain
That is curdling his heart, and distracting his brain ;
Then the vision shall change, and the darkness of
    night
Shall be lit by the flames of a red fitful light,
And the house he inhabits shall totter and shake,
Then away we will fly, as with screams he shall
    wake."

" This night, sister Fay, with its moonlight is ours,
We will drink the bright dew-drops that spangle
    the flowers ;
When the nightingale wakens the echoes around,
With our harps we will lengthen the languishing
    sound ;

Then, again, to the couch of the sleeper repair,
To the merchant, whose forehead is wrinkled with
    care,
And present to his view, in the silence of night,
His ships on the sea, in a desolate plight."

In his sleep he shall hear the bold mariner shout,
" Cut the cable and tack, the winds' veering about,
We must lighten the cargo, bring up from the hold
The stores, let them perish, life's dearer than gold ;"
Shall believe that he strives to outbellow the blast,
While his ingots and bales, in the waters are cast,
Then we'll spread on his lips, the white tips of our
    wings,
Till he starts, while his hands he with agony
    wrings.

" But softly, sweet sister, I hear on the gale,
The half stifled sighs of that artist so pale,
On the easel a portrait unfinished is spread,
While he dreams of the eyes he must paint in the
    head.
We must teach him the colors he nicely shall blend,
And the strokes it requires to accomplish his end,
Look, look, sister Fay, at his half lifted head,
And observe the bright smile o'er his countenance
    spread."

" Where the Poet is sleeping, again we will rest,
And a kiss on his lips shall in token be prest ;
And the theme of his song when his eye-lids unclose,
Shall be the bright dream that now breaks his repose.

That kiss on his lips shall a talisman prove,
And his numbers shall flow with the legends of love,
Till the hearts of his hearers acknowledge the spell—
But the daylight is breaking—sweet sister, fare-
    well.''

THE SONG OF THE GIPSY GIRL.

My home is in the wild wood,
    Beneath the old oak tree,
I know not what the luxury,
    Of covered roof may be ;
Yet well I love my canvas tent,
    For wheresoe'er I roam,
With lightsome heart I raise its shade,
    And call the place my home.

I love the breath of early dawn,
    When the lark is heard on high,
I love to watch the fleecy clouds,
    That float in the summer sky;
There may be joy in the city's din,
    But not for our ancient line,
Give me the crackling fire at eve,
    A wandering life be mine !

This nut-brown hand hath oft been sought,
    But I cannot leave my race,
There have been those who praised my form,
    My sparkling eyes and face ;

But I'd rather weave me a wreath of May
    To bind my raven hair,
Then win the softest silken snood,
    That high-born maidens wear.

I can braid my hair by yon silver stream,
    My vaulted roof the sky,
Can dance and sing 'neath the moon's pale beam,
    And swift the moments fly:
Then, why should I leave the gay green wood,
    For the city's stately walls,
The stars of Heaven, the song of birds,
    For cold and cheerless halls?

WHAT IS POETRY?

It is a spell of magic power,
A charm to soothe a lonely hour,
A silver veil o'er the human soul,
Binding the senses in sweet control;
A perfume, on life's dreary waste,
By radiant wings of Angels cast;
A rainbow in a clouded sky,
Pure as a beauteous vestal's sigh,
Ere the first blight of grief or care,
Hath cast a shade on her forehead fair.

Joyous as childhood's summer day,
It smiles 'midst the earliest bloom of May;
It scents the gale, when the fragrant rose
With regal beauty its leaves unclose ;
It hides with the violet in leafy dell,
And sleeps in the snowy lily bell ;
It rides o'er the fields, when the ripening corn
Is bent by the wind at early dawn ;
It laughs with the rustic in sultry June,
Beneath the beams of the silver moon.

It glows with the stars in the welkin high,
And gleams with the sun in the vaulted sky;
It trembles amid the wintry blast,
When its chains are over the waters cast ;
It blends with the shades of evening gray,
And floats on the breeze, with the lightest lay
That human lips have ever breathed,
'Midst every scene is its magic wreathed ;
It speaks to the heart in whispers bland,
And few its witchery can withstand.

It soothes the mournful soul to rest ;
Brings balm to the sufferer's aching breast ;
It flashes where mirth is wild and loud,
And blends with the shouts of the jovial crowd ;
It floats with the numbers that music flings,
With the incense of flowers, the breath of Spring,

The night-birds cry in the leafy grove,
When the moon is bright, and the fairies rove,
In the sunlight of summer, or winter's blast,
O'er every gem is its radiance cast!

———

NIGHT.

The mists are asleep on the hill,
Night's shadows are closing around;
The murmurs of streamlet and rill
Are heard with a whispering sound;
The peasant hath sunk to repose,
No light can be seen in the vale,
Where the nightingale breathes to the rose
Its plaintive and often-told tale!

Oh! this is the scene and the hour,
That are sacred to dreams of the past,
'Tis now that the absent have power
To rivet their fetters more fast:
The lost and the loved ones appear,
All faultless they rise on the sight,
Oh! memory thy visions are dear,
When felt in the calm hours of Night!

SEPTEMBER.

Like a nymph with golden hair
Clustering round her forehead fair,
And buskin to resist the morning dew,
   With reaping hook in hand,
   Doth fair September stand,
Looking on the earth with eyes like violets blue.

Eyes that never have been wet
With the teardrops of regret,
Lips still smiling with the songs of harvest home,
   Cheeks whose rosy blushes seem
   The reflection of a dream,
And shoulders white as is the ocean's foam.

She hath passed o'er field and plain,
And hath seen the golden grain,
Safely housed, and 'neath the forest trees has smiled
   At the schoolboys' shouts of glee
   As from the burthened tree
The many colored nuts have been despoiled.

The swallows' sad farewell
Sound like a funeral knell,
As they beat the ambient air with rapid wings;
  They no longer here will stay,
  But again in budding May
Their return to all a genial welcome brings.

  The summer flowers are dead,
  But the branches overhead,
Where so lately danced the leaves upon the trees
  In the softest hues of green,
  That adorn the sylvan scene,
Now in varied colors flutter in the breeze.

  Soon, too soon, upon the ground
  Will their resting-place be found,
Like a carpet for October's hurrying tread,
  When the rain-storms gathering sound
  Shall awake the echoes round,
As if mourning for the fair September dead.

THINK OF ME.

On the sea, on the sea, when the white spray is
      dancing,
  And the winds are at rest, will you think of me
      then?
When the planet of night is resplendently glancing,
  And the glow-worm hath lighted its lamp in the
      glen;

When lonely and sad, your rapt spirit is seeking,
    Midst dreams of the past, an elysium of bliss,
Like the rays that the rippling waters are breaking,
    In moments as clouded and changeful as this.

On the sea, on the sea, when the morning sun
    glistens,
    And the plashing of waters is murmuring round,
When your matins arise will you call down a bless-
    ing,
    Whose charm from the depths of the waters shall
        sound ?
Will you think on the lone one who turns from the
    coldness
    And scorn of this world with a feeling of pain,
Too proud to contend with, or shrink from the bold-
    ness,
    That blighted the roses on life's magic chain ?

On the sea, on the sea, when the sunbeams look
    brightest,
    And Hope is the spirit that rides on the wave,
Give a sigh and a tear, when your spirit is lightest,
    To the sorrows that sleep in the heart's burning
        grave.
And when you are lonely recall the affection
    That soothed your light sorrows and shared in
        your glee,
Our friendship was pure, and the sweet recollection
    Shall assuage the regret of this parting from thee.

THE YOUNG WIFE.

I listened for a foot-fall,
   When the silver moon shone bright,
And heeded not the splendor
   Of that unclouded night;
The little stars, like golden lamps,
   Hung in the vaulted sky,
But I only knew the one I loved,
   Was quickly drawing nigh.

The summer wind sighed mournfully
   As it whispered to the trees,
Still fresh with the perfume of flowers,
   Was that refreshing breeze;
But I only felt his warm caress,
   The pressure of his hand;
I only heard his gentle voice
   In whispers soft and bland.

I had loved him in my girlhood,
   Ere I knew that passion's power,
And everything he deigned to praise,
   Was sacred from that hour;
He never said, "he loved me,"
   When the rich and gay were loud
In praises of my mien and face,—
   A vile and sordid crowd—

He never said, "he loved me,"
  When my hand was wildly sought
By venal hearts, whose ready vows
  My glittering gold had caught;
But when my wealth had vanished,
  And I their coldness proved,
He sought alone to win my heart;
  'Twas then, he said "he loved."

He sought me in my loneliness,
  When reason's gentle voice
Proclaimed his worth—and proud I was
  To be his early choice;
My heart full long had been his own,
  And now my willing hand
I freely gave,—the only wealth
  I had at my command.

And now at the still evening hour,
  With all a matron's pride,
I listen for his welcome voice
  Beside our own fireside;
There have been those who sought me harm,
  But they have missed their end;
I once was lonely on this earth,
  But now I have a friend.

With his dear hand within my own,
  I feel the magic power
Of the radiant moon's resplendent light,
  At evening's mystic hour;

The perfumed gales, the glittering stars,
  The joys of sense and sight,
I feel and own their influence
  'With a thrill of glad delight!

Let those whose lives are passed in crowds,
  Despise my humble state,
There may be passion in their halls,
  But Love flies from the great;
He seeks the calm, sequestered vale,
  The poor man's lowly home,
And there he folds his silken wings,
  Without a wish to roam.

THEY ARE NO MORE.

They are no more! the various joys of youth—
  Fled with the smiles that then were early beam-
    ing,
They are no more! those dreams of love and truth
  That then our young fond hearts were wildly
    dreaming;
The very friends, that were so good and kind,
  Fortune, neglect, or death, had power to sever,
And we no more the links can fondly bind,
  Or deem those ties will prove our own forever.

Oh! what a happy, glorious world was this,
  Our hearts the founts from which its light was
        beaming,
Our very life, was then a source of bliss,
  As of a happier future we were dreaming;
Childhood and youth, too quickly do ye fly,
  Manhood hath cares for all its coming hours,
Change after change, in vain, in vain we try,
  And still the thorns are oftener seen than flowers.

Love, fame and fortune, each a varied track,
  That in the distance show so goodly fair,
When these are gained, we still a something lack,
  To chase the deep'ning furrows time will wear:
The first, a vapor of the lightest kind,
  That round our path its various arts unfold,
And fame, and fortune, we too often find
  Are splendid chains, that bind the human soul.

Thus, step by step, we tread this mortal coil,
  And one by one, its glories fade from view,
Still onward, onward, with unceasing toil,
  Some meteor of an hour we still pursue.
We live, we move, we fret our little span,
  We die, and are to kindred earth returned,
Such is the glorious heritage of Man,
  Known for a moment, for a moment mourned.

TO "ANNIE."

It is not lonely thus to watch
    The fading days decline,
For other thoughts I dash aside,
    And my soul speaks to thine;
I will not dwell on far off scenes,
    They sadden all my rhymes—
The *present* shall my pen employ,
    Away with by-gone times !

You say your homestead fields are fair,
    Your homestead woods are green
And bright, as when I wandered there,
    Pleased with their leafy screen ;
The landscape shines before me now,
    Bright with the golden grain,
And now a hill, and now a dale,
    And now a fertile plain.

The bay sweeps by majesticly
    And white sails gleam thereon ;
How oft we've watched those snowy sails,
    And numbered every one?
And the dark hills beyond the coast
    Looked frowning o'er the deep,
As if to chide these swan-like sails,
    For their quiet, dream-like sleep.

I know you love these fruitful scenes,
　　And every spot is dear,
And I believe they are as fair
　　As when I wandered there;
As when I sang old songs to thee,
　　Or spoke in wayward rhymes,
The snatches of those endless tales,
　　That told of happier times!

Old songs, old friends and by-gone times,
　　All memories of the past,
I exorcise ye from my heart,
　　Round which your chains are cast!
I break the spell,—away, I'm free!
　　And lo! a lonely room
Within an ancient mansion's walls,
　　That now I call my own.

The taper glimmers by my side,
　　Dark is the evening sky;
No star hath shown its cherub face
　　To glad the vault on high;
It is not lonely thus to watch
　　The fading day's decline,
For then my restless spirit loves
　　To breathe its dreams to thine!

7

A SERMON IN VERSE.

THE POOR.

" The poor you have always with ye."

Oh ! deem not the poor an alien race,
    Speak not of their woes with scorn ;
Let not disdain overshadow your face
    When those who are needy—mourn !
They toil, and complain not, from morn till night,
    On the soil, in mines, or in mills.
Oh ! rich man, pity their hapless plight,
    And seek to redress their ills !

They ask but for work, that their children dear
    And wives may not faint and die,
And an Angel records each sufferer's prayer
    In the Book that is sealed on High.
Our God hath said, that from the store
    The rich man claims alone,
A part shall be given to the poor,
    And the debt shall be His own.

'Tis little they ask,—their daily bread,
  For which they with joy will toil.
With plenty the rich man's board is spread
  From the produce of the soil,
That the hardy laborer's care hath won ;—
  Then why should the wealthy claim
The sweets,—not labor,—for their own,
  When *all* should share the same ?

Give work, give bread, with liberal hand,
  Remember the Judgment Seat,
Where the rich and poor together shall stand,
  And their future doom await.
'Tis here alone we can place on High
  Resources to meet that day,
When Christ shall appear in Majesty,
  And this earth shall pass away.

Where then shall the Palace rear its head,
  When the Mighty of the land,
With trembling forms and shrieks of dread
  Shall beside the lowliest stand ?
Peasant and prince in one mingled crowd
  Shall await their eternal doom,
The lowly and mean, the high and the proud,
  Must alike to judgment come.

On earth the poor have kindred dear,
    Who look to them for bread,
Whose is the blame, and whose the care,
    That they are so barely fed?
Alike we tread one common earth,
    Worship one Holy God,
From the same source obtain our birth,
    Shall rot 'neath the self-same sod!

Then deem not the Poor an alien race,
    Speak not of their wants with scorn,
Let not disdain overshadow your face
    When those who are needy mourn!

OCTOBER.

Bright are the tresses that cover her bosom,
  Brighter the brown cheek the 'sunbeam hath
    kissed,
As lightly she moves, scarcely bending a blossom,
  Fair queen of the woodland, bright child of the
    mist.

The rowan tree offers its berries to crown her,
  The "hip and the haw" the same homage de-
    signed,
The purple grapes are the bright gems that October
Entwines with the acorn, her temples to bind.

Adown the green pasture, across the steep mountain,
  She airily floats like a bird on the wing,
And then on the margin of river and fountain
  She rests, till the zephyrs her madrigal sing.

She touches the branches of maple and willow,
   And with joy every leaflet returns the salute,
Softly blending their hues, with the sound of -the
     billow,
   Whilst the songsters in forest and woodland are
     mute.

The ground is half covered with leaves lately falling,
   That rustle and laugh as she passeth along,
The wild winds of autumn are mournfully calling,
   Now loudly—then soft—as the nightingale's song.

The schoolboy his holliday spends in the wild wood,
   Where the squirrel is busy collecting his store,
Whilst the birdling whose legend enchanted our
     childhood
   Shyly comes, as of old, to the cottager's door,—

The robin,—who first woke the echoes with gladness,
   Who called to the daisies, and bid them appear,
Now. sings, though his song hath the low notes of
     sadness,
   As he swings on the trees growing leafless and
     bare.

"LET THE DEAD PAST BURY THE DEAD."

My Annie, when the present bears
    Its own fantastic sway,
Why will you seek the dreamy past
    To chase its smiles away?
Each moment that to us is lent
    Still bears upon its track,
A host of feelings, griefs and joys,
    Then why should we look back?
The hours that were, the hours that are,
    Have each their hues of light,
Blended amidst the weariness
    That hung upon their flight.

So, when a child the rainbow sees
    Descending from the skies,
To win the many colored band
    He with impatience flies;
But as he strives to gain the hill
    Where it appeared to rest,
He sees the object of his search
    Gleam on the mountain's breast.
We laugh at the aspiring child,
    And know his search is vain,
For, could he climb the mountain's brow,
    He'd see it on the plain.

So 'tis with us when we would blend
    Amidst our present ill,
The saddest memories of the past,
    And brood upon them still.
Look round, and bless the Power that gives
    Each moment of our time,
And learn to guard the treasure well
    In every scene and clime :
The past should teach us how to bear
    The trials of our lot,
By pointing out, in dangers past,
    We were not quite forgot !
Should teach us that no joy can last,
    No grief can long remain—
As sunshine follows darkest night,
    As joy succeeds to pain.

Suppose we lose a favorite friend
    By death or human art,
Some other fills the lost one's place
    Within our changeful heart.
Should wealth be spent, or, worse than all,
    Should we be left forlorn,
Time is the power that binds our wounds,
    Then wherefore should we mourn ?
Wreathe, wreathe the present but with smiles,
    And lift the heart on high—
And for the past, my pensive friend,
    No longer will you sigh !

DEATH AT SEA.

The gallant bark was homeward bound,
  But death was busy there,
And nought availed the Doctor's aid
  To obstruct his fell career ;
The sick man bent his stately head
  His comrade's arm beside,
He whispered of home with failing breath,
  And on the ocean died.

The restless waters dashed around,
  When his sorrowing comrades gave
At the midnight watch reluctantly,
  His body to the grave ;
No sculptured urn records his worth ;
  No holy words were said,
As the waves closed over the breathless clay,
  From which the soul had fled.

Old ocean, what sad tales of woe,
  Thy voice breathes through the soul,
As boldly thou lifts thy giant foam,
  Defying all control !
Ah ! who can reflect on the hidden graves,
  Without a silent prayer,
For the souls of those whose cold remains
  Are deeply buried there.

7*

TO "ANNIE."

It is not lonely thus to watch
  The fading days decline,
For other thoughts I dash aside,
  And my soul speaks to thine ;
I will not dwell on far off scenes,
  They sadden all my rhymes—
The *present* shall my pen employ,
  Away with by-gone times !

You say your homestead fields are fair,
  Your homestead woods are green
And bright, as when I wandered there,
  Pleased with their leafy screen ;
The landscape shines before me now,
  Bright with the golden grain,
And now a hill, and now a dale,
  And now a fertile plain.

The bay sweeps by majesticly
  And white sails gleam thereon ;
How oft we've watched those snowy sails,
  And numbered every one?
And the dark hills beyond the coast
  Looked frowning o'er the deep,
As if to chide these swan-like sails,
  For their quiet, dream-like sleep.

I know you love these fruitful scenes,
  And every spot is dear,
And I believe they are as fair
  As when I wandered there ;
As when I sang old songs to thee,
  Or spoke in wayward rhymes,
The snatches of those endless tales,
  That told of happier times !

Old songs, old friends and by-gone times,
  All memories of the past,
I exorcise ye from my heart,
  Round which your chains are cast !
I break the spell,—away, I'm free !
  And lo ! a lonely room
Within an ancient mansion's walls,
  That now I call my own.

The taper glimmers by my side,
  Dark is the evening sky;
No star hath shown its cherub face
  To glad the vault on high ;
It is not lonely thus to watch
  The fading day's decline,
For then my restless spirit loves
  To breathe its dreams to thine !

7

No wonder that his cheek grew pale,
   His manly eye grew dim,
As he knew that old familiar place,
   Was now, no home for him !
Oh ! there are pages in life's book
   That nothing can erase,
And scenes,—that plant the seeds of care,
   Upon the human face :

Take from the heart the bounding pulse,
   With which it used to glow,
And blend amidst all after joys,
   The cankering roots of woe !
He turned him from the garden stile
   And blest the solitude,
That reigned around,—no friend or foe,
   Did on his grief intrude.

He stood alone ! who once was blest
   With kindred hearts and warm,
The last of all his race on earth,
   To meet the gathering storm ;
He who had basked in fortune's rays
   With light and gleeful heart,
He who had seen by slow degrees,
   Her blessings all depart ;

He who had never sought for gold,
　With narrow soul to hoard,
Who had been generous in the days
　When plenty blest his board ;
When sorrow came,—with manly brow,
　He hid the cankered dart,
And few could scan the secret woe,
　Of his firm, enduring heart.

He stood alone ! the wintry winds,
　Sung with their own wild mirth,—
To take a lingering last Farewell,
　Of the place that saw his birth.
To-morrow, these soft clinging thoughts
　Must be indulged no more,
He then must walk the lonely deck,
　And brave the ocean's roar.

Self-exiled from his native land,
　He then must learn to bear,
The bondage of a servant's state,—
　Who once was master here :
Well 'tis alone,—he meets the blow,
　Well 'tis alone,—he wept,
There had been deeper woe for him,
　Had not his loved ones slept.

I speak not of the summer friends,
  That change when storms come on,
But of the dead,— whose quiet graves,
  He sadly thinks upon :
His faithful wife,—his cherub boy,—
  His parents good and kind,—
Theirs were the hearts that to his own,
  Grief had now closely twined :

Theirs were the smiles that rendered Home,
  A paradise to him,
And half the sighs that now he breathes,
  Are orisons for them.
Slowly he passed the church-yard path,
  Where side by side they lay,
Wife—home—and country now Farewell—
  He said, and turned away !

            *   *   *   *   *

      Many eyes are weary,
        Still they fondly gaze,
      On the fast receding lands,
        The scenes of other days ;
      On the valley's shadowy streams,
        On the mountain's crown,
      On the quiet hamlet,
        On the busy town.

Gaily o'er the waters
  Bounds the stately bark
In which their world of wealth is stored
  To them a second Ark,
The land they sadly gaze upon,
  Its mountains, rocks, and streams,
Often now shall visit them,
  In their nightly dreams.

Some have sighed at parting,
  Others wildly wept,
Still the vessel breasts the waves,
  As its onward course it kept.
Who is he, that stands alone,
  With calm unruffled mien,
Whose air and garb bespeak him one,
  That better days hath seen?
All the tedious voyage
  He seeks no converse there,
And never mingles with the throng
  Save at the hour of prayer.
Gaily o'er the deep blue sea,
  The gallant ship speeds on
Until the far-off land they seek,
  Is gladly gazed upon.

*   *   *   *   *

Build we a home where the surges are singing
  Or where the wild stretches lonely and sear,
There 'tis our heart's best affections are clinging,
  There 'tis we fain would place those that are dear.
Sad is the lone of heart, weary his waking,
  Who hath no kindly hand clasped in his own,
Who hath no dear one when all else forsake him,
  Who in sunshine or sorrow clings to him alone.

*   *   *   *   *   *

Again a home is his,—
  Where Columbia's mountains frown,
Where trackless plains, deep forest shades,
  And torrents wild abound ;
Again a home is his,—
  Well suited to his soul,
Lonely and cheerless, wild and sad,
  Unlike his home of old.

Upon his high and manly brow,
  Is seen the shade of care,
And 'midst his clustering locks of brown,
  The silver threads appear.
A lonely and a saddened heart,
  Finds solitude its balm,
Though time but slowly drags its chain,
  In such a state of calm.

Spring threw her sweets with liberal hand
    Around his cottage door ;
When summer suns grew warm and bright
    His heart was glad once more ;
He learnt to love the restless life
    That now he had to lead,
And as his heart again beat glad,
    Time flew with quickened speed.

He turned with chastened love to Him,
    Who rules the earth and skies
And who ordained the sun alike
    On good and bad to rise ;
He learnt to bless the Power that ruled
    His lowly changeful lot,
To worship Him, with faith and love,
    And half his cares forgot.

A voice is heard, amidst the breeze
    Of penitence and prayer,
Each falling leaf speaks to his soul,
    The balm of peace is there :
Again with cheerful heart he rose,
    Once more his voice is gay,
With calmer mood he calls to mind
    The scenes of yesterday.

His flocks increase, his garden gleams,
   With many an English flower,
His orchard boughs bend with the fruit,
   A good and welcome store ;
Years, years of hardy toil have passed,
   And home is home again,
As dear as that which long ago,
   Rose on Old England's plain.

And he hath found another mate,
   Whose smiles repay his toil,
And hardy sons are by his side,
   When working on the soil :
And when the birds awake the morn,
   Their voices sweetly blend,
With the matin songs of praise and prayer,
   That then to Heaven ascend.

Sweet is the social hour of eve,
   When round the hearth they press,
To listen to some tales of joy,
   Or themes that breathe distress ;
There are no joys upon this earth,
   Compared with those of home,
Where sire and children sweetly dwell,
   Without a wish to roam.

NOVEMBER.

November old, with garments thin,
    And scanty locks of silver hair,
Stands leaning on his pilgrim staff,
    In the cold and frosty midnight air.
He has wrapped his robe about his form,
    And at the casement whispers low,
Take pity on a poor old man
    Oppressed with care and woe !

Where'er I pass the doors are closed,
    The casements fastened down,
I ask relief from door to door,
    But am answered with a frown ;
I wave my hand, and the winds arise,
    With loud and lusty cry;
And the rain falls down, over city and town,
    From the dark and lowering sky.

Open the door, for the crystal hail
  Strikes keenly through my garments thin;
The smiling lamp and ruddy fire
  Make glad the rooms you sit within;
And the softened strains from voice and lute
  Chime sweetly with the rushing gale,
I am waiting for an entrance here,
  For pity hear an old man's tale.

The waning year is near its close,
  Hath rung its changes far and wide,
Old Christmas hides in an icy cave,
  You will welcome him with generous pride;
And dress your halls with the holly bough,
  And your friends will come from far and near,
And drink your health in a flowing bowl,
  And praise your liberal Christmas cheer!

I shall pass away, and my funeral pall
  Will dissolve with the rush of the pelting shower;
The wind my requiem psalm will sing,
  When the darkest night shall grimly lower;
And the icy breath of the frozen lake,
  Shall hang on the boughs of the leafless trees,
And the wild storm swell, over moor and fell,
  And shout my name to the wintry breeze,

I am old and poor, and my breath is short,
  And my trembling limbs are scantly clad;
My locks are gray, and my voice is hoarse,
  And my farewell song is lorn and sad.

I came with kindly hopes and fears
   And waited long at your window pane ;
But you gave no heed to my mournful tale
   So " fare you well," till we meet again.

————

FADING LEAVES.

The autumn leaves of crimson, brown and gold,
   Are clinging to the shivering branches yet ;
Soon they will rustle on the dark, damp mould,
   Reminding us of scenes we would forget ;
Scenes of the past, long banished from our view,
   Its trials and temptations, pains and cares,
With the bland influence of the trusted few,
   Whose watchful kindness wiped away our tears.

In the glad spring-time hope holds carnival,
   We hail the infant year with zeal and joy;
Rejoicing in the charms of hill and dale,
   Gives life a zest time never can destroy.
Who thinks of " fading leaves " when the soft green
   Peeps from the branches of our favorite trees ?
Or, of brown autumn's tears in the soft sheen
   That lights the boughs and trembles in the breeze ?

When summer days are warm and nights are clear,
    Leaves, flowers, and fruits, to full perfection
        brought,
In the refulgence of the glowing year
    To fading leaves we seldom give a thought.
The earth is clothed with verdure, and the shade
    Of the dark forest trees refreshment brings;
The song-birds' nests are in the branches made,
    We hear the fluttering of their restless wings.

When autumn enters what a change appears,
    The leaves are altering every eve and morn,
The varied livery which the season wears,
    From the tall poplar to the lowly thorn;
The pale sad flowers that linger for awhile
    Are quite outshone, outnumbered by the leaves
That in their changeful beauty seem to smile
    Before they fall and perish in their graves.

The sunlight smiles upon these "fading leaves,"
    The wind is singing them a farewell hymn,
The silver moon looks sadly on their graves,
    And on their beauty that is waning dim.
Soon the bare branches will look stern and cold,
    Only the fir and ivy clothed in green—
These through all seasons do their colors hold,
    The hardy veterans of the woodland scene.

"MELANCHOLY DAYS."

Over hill and dale, over land and sea,
  The wind is singing a requiem wild
To the leaves that fall from the woodland tree,
  With a wailing cry, like a weeping child ;
And the withering leaves, with a rustling sound,
  Respond to the mournful lullaby;
They dance for a while on the damp, cold ground,
  And are kissed by the moaning wind ere they die !

The zephyrous gales in the summer's prime,
  When the green leaves covered the wild bird's nest,
Rang merrily forth in the joyous chime,
  With the lay of the birds they rocked to rest.
And the songsters on the blossoming spray,
  'Mid the chorus of the genial breeze,
When Nature's face was bright and gay,
  Had no fear of days, " so mournful " as these.

The wind is at war with the pelting rain,
  Drifting the sleet o'er the desolate moor,
Dashing the spray on the window pane,
  Driving the snow to the cottager's door ;
And it howls in its wrath like a wolf at bay,
  Through the dreary hours of the wintry night,
Till, like the giants of old, at play,
  Its course can be traced in the morning light.

Who can tell the form of the wind?
    Or its pathway trace on earth—in air—
What mighty spell can its pinions bind,
    So restlessly fluttering everywhere?
As over the loftiest mountain it sweeps,
    Drinking the dew from the herbs and flowers,
Or along the lowliest valley it creeps,
    Rifling the sweets of the vernal bowers.

PRIDE: A FABLE.

A spider in a lofty hall
Had spun his web from wall to wall,
And warily watching from day to day,
For the insects that became its prey:
"I am a monarch," the spider sung,
As its web on the shining wall was hung,
"Many slaves on earth there be,
But I dwell aloft, secure and free."

A rook had built on a towering tree,
Caw-cawed to its mate right merrily;
"See how our nest rocks with the wind,
We are out of the reach of human kind,
No school-boy can climb to our home on high,
We almost seem to touch the sky;
Here, we will rear our progeny;
And they like us, will be safe and free."

A lark from the dewy grass arose,
Singing its vespers at evening's close;
Higher and higher, ascended the bird,
Louder and sweeter, its notes were heard,
Like a seraph's song were its warblings clear,
As it hung like a note in the summer air;
"I rise above all others," sang he,
"On earth or in air, I am safe and free."

An eagle sat in his eyrie high,
Like a dark shadow, against the sky;
Safely its young ones looked around,
On the gleaming of the untrodden ground,
The foot of man had never prest
The height on which was built its nest;
King of the solitude he seemed to be,
As he screamed aloud, "I am safe and free."

MORAL.

"Boastful Pride hath often a fall!"
The spider was swept from the lofty wall,
The nest of the rook fell to the ground,
Where its dusty progeny were found;
The tuneful lark by the fowler was slain,
Its life-blood scattered like ruby rain;
And the eagle was brought from its eyrie high,
And ended its days in captivity.

8

THE INDIAN SUMMER.

She appears on earth like an Eastern Queen,
  With star-gemmed dusky hair,
As pure and calm as the silver moon
  That floats in ethereal air.

Her regal train trails over the plain,
  Wet with the dew-drops bright;
Her light bound scarcely touching the ground
  As she takes her ærial flight.

She smiles, and Nature blushes with joy;
  She sings, and the zephyrs sigh;
The fading flowers uplift their heads
  To bless her ere they die.

She hath chained the frost in his icy cave,
  And the wild winds fastened down,
Our dusky Empress' reign is short,
  Yet she fears no tyrant's frown.

Now over the landscape silence falls,
  And over the waters clear,
The quiet that soothes the mourner's soul
  With her reign will disappear.

Her dirge will be sung by the evening gale,
  Her funeral pall the snow ;
And the rhyme of the wave shall ring o'er her grave
  As the waters ebb and flow.

The Spring and Summer flowers are dead,
  And the Autumn's golden store
Has been gathered from orchard, field, and wold,
  And her busy days are o'er.

And when Winter old, with his coat of mail,
  Shall have bound the gentle stream,
The Indian Summer's golden days
  Will appear like a fairy dream.

————

"BOYS WILL BE BOYS."

Fred, Harry and Tom have returned from school ;
  Just hark to their almost deafening noise ;
There is no such thing as order and rule
  In a house that's tormented with rollicking boys ;
And poor grandmama, who loves them so well,
  Has scarcely a moment of quiet or rest,
So many demands on her patience and time,
  Her life is a hurry-and-worry at best.

The rocking-horse soon is minus a leg,
  The drum's given out with a hole in its side,
The new set of books are tattered and torn,
  The strings of the kite are tangled and tied.
Always in mischief from morning till night,
  The noisiest youngsters under the sun,
Yet to hear the excuses grandmama makes,
  You would think they were models, every one.

A house full of boys let loose from school,
  I certainly think would provoke a saint;
They litter the kitchen, parlor and hall,
  Spoil the carpets and paper, and dirty the paint;
It is no use complaining, for grandmama
  Appears to enjoy their wearisome noise,
And if I correct them,—as sometimes I do,—
  She scolds and persistently sides with the boys.

And thus she continues, and argues the case,
  "I know they are healthy and robust and strong,
Can run, shout and whistle, are careless and gay,
  And cut up their capers all the day long;
Bright eyes, rosy cheeks, are sufficient excuse
  For deafening noises, torn books, broken toys,
You must really have patience," is grandmama's
    cry,
  And remember the adage, that "Boys will be
    boys."

THE CURSE OF GOLD.

Thou art a bride, sweet maiden, and thy face is very
  fair,
And well that wreath of orange bloom becomes thy
  raven hair ;
But wherefore art thou pale, dear girl, why doth
  the tear-drop flow,
Can there be sadness in thy heart ; what dost thou
  dream on now ?
Why do you sigh, why do you weep, why shun
  your husband's kiss ?
Your lips have breathed the earnest vow that made
  you wholly his ?
Say, is it maiden modesty that makes you turn aside,
Lest he should press your trembling hand, who are
  his new-made bride?

A broken ring—a faded flower—a tress of golden
  hair—
Are these the tokens of a love once to your memory
  dear ?
The Past !   What hours of glad delight are breathing near you now,
When your heart owned a dearer love and vowed a
  different vow !

Those pearls are bright that bind your arm; you are
    a rich man's bride,
For wealth you left your earliest love,—more dear
    than aught beside;
Go dry those tears,—go hush those sighs,—they
    must not see you weep;
The wakeful vigil of despair your heart in pain
    shall keep.

Thou now art fair, sweet maiden,—but thy lip will
    lose its red,
And who can call the roses back that from thy
    cheek have fled;
Alas! that human hearts should bleed at the de-
    mon-shrine of pride!
I envy not thy brilliant lot, thou young and lovely
    bride;
The memory of a broken heart shall haunt thee in
    thy sleep,
As even now you turn aside in solitude to weep;
The wealth for which thy hand is sold can never
    bring repose,
To thee it hath less value now, than that once
    blooming rose.

DECEMBER.

Keen blows the angry wind,
 And the snow-wreath is seen,
Bleak is the prospect on upland and lea ;
 Leafless the forest tree,
 Lately so fresh and green,
Still there is music, wild, wandering free.

 Hark ! to the torrent's roar,
 O'er the smooth pebbles play,
List to the spirit-like song of the leaf ;
 Chainless the first dash on,
 Making unearthly moan,
Such is our tide of life, fleeting and brief.

 Now the bright flowers are dead,
 And the wild birds have fled,
Bring the old holly branch home to your door ;
 Now 'tis the evergreen,
 Laurel and bay are seen—
Bind the glad Christmas wreath gaily once more.

Let the wind roar without,
Drifting the fallen snow,
Where the warm fire glows little we care ;
Safe by the ingle-side,
Where joy and mirth preside,
Merry laugh, song and jest, gaily we share.

FAITH, HOPE AND CHARITY.

Three virtues abide, brighter far than the sun,
Or anything earthly the sun shines on,—
Faith, Hope and Charity, mystical three,
" But the greatest of these is Charity !"

FAITH.

The first of these virtues is holy Faith !
Like a radiant crown,
As hath ever been shown,
It encircles our temples in life or death ;
And unless this radiant crown be obtained,
The love of the Father can not be retained
Our efforts, our hopes, expectations will fail,
Even-all our good works will nothing avail ;
For the same inspiration has written the word,
" Without Faith 'tis impossible man can please
God !"

HOPE.

Hope, like an anchor on which to rest,
   Changes to joy our sorrowful tears ;
'Tis a spirit that soothes our soul's unrest,
   And ever and always a calm front bears.
It whispers of happier days to come,
   Even when tempests our fears assail,
And we bend, expecting a heavier doom,
   As our eyes are dim and our cheeks are pale.
It points to the silver that lines the cloud,
   And gathers us softly within its arms,
Whispering gently, or breathing aloud
   The mystical word that our senses charms—
Faith is a seraph of heavenly birth,
Hope a bright spirit pertaining to earth.

CHARITY.

Emblem of patience, serene and calm,
For every evil a sovereign balm ;
Under all trials forgiving and kind,
No shade of suspicion obscuring the mind ;
Teaching poor mortals the purest Faith,
The veil that encircles us even in death ;
After our pilgrimage, when we rest,
And our bodies are hid in the earth's cold breast;
When the mission of Faith and Hope is past,
And we gaze on the Father's face at last :
  8*

If we the veil of Charity bring
To the presence of Heaven's omnipotent King,
Pure and unsullied from earthly stain,
It will show the brighter for all the pain,
For all the care, and sorrow, and loss,
Then we shall joyfully look on the cross
On which for man the Saviour died,
To put to shame all worldly pride.
We have, on earth, been true to the last,
And for us its trials and sorrows are past ;
Still abideth the mystical three,
" But the greatest of these is Charity."

———

THE HEART'S SHRINE.

What heart but bears a secret shrine,
Round which its best affections twine?
Some treasured record of the past,
Hath o'er it, its reflection cast,
With just sufficient shade to show
Joy hath brief dwelling place below,
And just enough of light to prove
How cheering is the smile of love.

Oh, every human heart hath ties
Time cannot sever as it flies !
The joyous laugh of childhood's day,
With sunny youth may pass away,
And manhood's life flit swiftly past,
And many griefs their shadows cast
Upon the gems and flowers of earth,
That shed their gladness o'er our path.

The springing step, the actions wild,
That well became the playful child,
As years increase may, too, depart,
As colder grows the human heart.
Still memory keeps its secret shrine,
Unchill'd by years, untouched by time,
Dear to us when our skies are fair,
When storms assail us still more dear. .

The lonely hermit in his cell,
With "sandal-shoon, and scallop shell,"
Who lives apart from all that brings
Remembrance of life's fleeting things,
Whose steadfast soul is vowed to Him
That died to save the world from sin,
Why doth he fly all earthly love?
Because his *shrine* is fixed above.

Yon siren who, amidst the throng,
Pours the enchantment of her song—
What is it gives her heart the tone?
'Tis the sweet music of her home:
She sees not those who stand around,
Her spirit lives on dearer ground!
Her song hath ceased, and o'er her brow
Remembrance casts its shadows now.

When life its glories sheds around,
And every spot seems fairy ground,
Where high-born lords and ladies fair,
Seem free from the fell demon, *Care.*
Oh! could we pierce the specious veils
That all their weariness conceals,
We less should grudge the envied state
And gaudy trammels of the great.

It is not every cheerful brow,
The heart's recess doth clearly show;
Not every lip that wears a smile,
Proves the heart's gladness by that wile;
For none but HE who reads the heart,
And nicely scans each hidden part,
Can tell how often smiles are worn,
To hide the ranklings of the thorn.

The sons of genius seldom find
Communion sweet with human kind;
Little they know of human love,
Though envy's shafts they often prove,
And coldly turn from crowds aside,
Or laugh to scorn the frowns of pride;
Nature for them her stores unfolds,
And fills with happiness their souls.

Their shrine is wreathed with every flower,
That blossoms for a sunny hour;
The song of birds, the hum of bees,
The sighing winds that sweep the seas,
The shades of night o'er moor and fell,
The sunlight gleaming in the dell,
Find echo in the Poet's heart,
And leave for Earth but little part.

The pilgrim on a lonely shore,
Who only hears the ocean roar
In answer to his lonely call,
Feels less of gloom pervade his soul,
Than he whose warmth of heart grows chill
By oft-repeated acts of ill,
Cast on him by his fellow worm,
Who cannot quell, though raise the storm.

The sailor on the chainless deep,
Keeps silent watch whilst others sleep;
Slowly he treads the deck, and feels
Kind, gentle thoughts around him steal;
Dreams of his home are hovering nigh,
Thoughts of the absent draw a sigh,
Wife, home, and children, each have part,
In the warm feelings of his heart.

The soldier on the tented field,
With stainless crest and burnished shield,
Clasps to his breast the lock of hair
His lady-love gave him to wear;
Her bright eyes are before him now,
Again he seems to hear the vow
She breathed at parting. Say, hath Time
The power to desecrate that shrine?

Oh! every heart its records keep
Some visions that will never sleep,
All other flowers may fade away,
One memory never knows decay:
Time deeper marks the impress there,
As drops of water stones will wear,—
Remembrance of our earliest love,
Will rise all other dreams above.

A FUNERAL DIRGE.

"In memoriam of the Most Reverend Archbishop Spalding."

Toll the bells in spire and tower,
   Drape the church in somber guise,
Let loving fingers touch the lyre,
   And bid the funeral chant arise!
Call around the sacred dead,
Those who have by *Him* been led,
Marshalled on in virtue's path,
With precepts far too pure for earth!

Let solemn canticles arise,
A spirit gains its Paradise!
A valiant soldier of the Cross,
His the gain and ours the loss!

Let the orphans sadly weep,
As the mournful watch they keep;
Let the students chant his praise,
In gentle sympathetic lays;
Let rich and poor, their sorrows blend,
For loss of Pastor, Father, Friend;
Whilst the Priests in sable stole,
Intone the "Requiem" for his soul!

In each fane he raised to win,
Our souls from falling into sin,
We, his children, kneel and raise,
Our souls to Heaven in mournful lays;
Let us not forget the care,
That built for us the house of prayer.

The " De Profundis " like a wail
From holy souls, shall there assail,
The tenderest thrill of human love,
And raise our minds to Heaven above.

And, as the chains that giants bind
Fall off, and leave them unconfined,
The prayers we offer in our zeal,
The tender pity that we feel,
Even the offering of our tears,
The incense of our fervent prayers,
Our alms and penitential sighs,
May for such souls to Heaven arise.
Those valiant soldiers of the Cross,
Theirs the gain and ours the loss !

Human love no floods can drown,
All are by its limits bound.
The purest offering it can share,
Is the blest sound of humblest prayer !

BETHLEHEM.

Virgins come ! a virgin calls you,
   Kneel down on the stable floor,
Be the first to greet the Saviour,
   Enter at the lowly door.
See the babe within the manger,
   Robed in snowy swaddling bands ;
Warm and smiling is the infant,
   Tended by the Virgin's hands.

Enter Mothers ! fear no danger,
   Angel bands are hovering near ;
All earth's children, guardian spirits,
   Circle round Creation's heir ;
No place for Him, in court or castle,
   No shelter from the winter's cold,
E'en within the lowliest cottage,
   As for ages hath been told.

Hasten Fathers ! leave your burthens,
   Cares, and trials, far behind,
Wait not for a second bidding,
   Here, you will compassion find ;
Here,—a balm for cares and crosses,
   Cast them at the Saviour's feet,
Be amongst the first adorers,
   That the Royal Infant greet.

Children come! he calls you to Him,
    Be not slow to do his will;
Bring your unstained first affections,
    Let your joy the stable fill.
Lift your voices in glad carols,
    Check no sigh—restrain no tear,
See the tender Mother watching,
    All are blest who enter here.

CHRISTMAS.

The laurel and holly, rosemary and bay,
    Are bright with the tears of falling showers,
Their leaves and red berries, dispute the sway,
    Of spring and summer's roseate flowers;
Full dearly we cherished each blossoming bough,
    When the hedge-rows were verdant in early spring
But winter hath fastened his fetters now,
    And other memories round us cling.

"Glory to God,—Peace to men of good-will,"
    Sang the Heavenly hosts on Bethlehem's plains,
To the Shepherds who watched, through the night
      hours still,
    "Rejoice for the Lord Eternal reigns."

" Glory and Peace,"—chants Holy Rood
    At morn, at noon, and at close of day,
And now we stand,—as the Shepherds stood,
    Like them we kneel, and homage pay.

In spirit we enter the stable door,
    To worship the King of Heaven and Earth,
We see the Shepherds so mean and poor,
    And the Virgin to whom He owed his birth,
The faithful Saint Joseph with staff in hand,
    The Babe Divine in the manger laid,
The ox, and the ass, beside Him stand
    As if to guard, both babe and maid.

Ages have passed,—still the joy-bells ring,
    Proclaiming to man, that "a Saviour is given,"
With carols we welcome the Infant King,
    Whose scepter extends over Earth and Heaven.
The young and the old, have counted the hours,
    And waited and watched for this festival day,
Then your homes to adorn,—instead of bright
       flowers,
    Take laurel and holly, rosemary and bay.

"GLORIA IN EXCELSIS DEO."

A CHRISTMAS HYMN.

Hark! the heavenly angel singeth,
  'Midst the brightness of the skies,
Peace on earth, to man he bringeth,
  Shepherds, fear not, but arise!
Tidings of great joy, are sounding
  From the golden harps on high;
Myriads of the heavenly army,
  Round the watchers soon draw nigh,
Telling them of signs and wonders,
  Of the Mother and the Son;
That the babe laid in the manger,
  And the King of Heaven are one!

  "Gloria in excelsis Deo!"
  Proclaimed on earth this holy morn;
  Hearken to the joyful canto—
  "To man, is now, a Saviour born!"

From the earth arose the Shepherds,
   Let us hasten each one said,
To the infant in the stable,
   Tended by the lowly maid!
For the sign from Heaven sent them,
   By the shining Angel band,
Tho' it filled their souls with rapture,
   Was hard for them to understand;
Yet they rose,—their flocks abandoned,
   All uncared for on the hill,
No one lingered,—no one doubted,
   Glad to do God's Holy will.

Soon they reached the lowly stable,
There the new-born infant see,
" Gloria in excelsis Deo,"—
Each one breathes on bended knee.

Faith sublime made clear the tidings,
   Erst so full of mystery,
Faith! which out of darkness light brings,
   Faith! which lives eternally.
Mary heard the humble Shepherds
   Speaking of the Angels bright,
And she pondered on the message,
   And the radiance of the light:

In her heart she hid the wonder,
 Bowed her head and kissed the child,
The Incarnate God,—the Saviour,
 Looked upon her face and smiled.

" Gloria in excelsis Deo,"
Peace on earth and joy in Heaven,
Unto Man, is born a Saviour,
To fallen Man, a King is given !

THE OLD YEAR.

The old year, slowly passing away,
Is palsied and tottering, worn and gray,
His form is bent, his footsteps slow,
His face is stained with tears of woe ;
Never again till Time lies dead,
Shall this "Old Year" lift up his head.

Farewell ! and may thy end be peace,
To one and all a glad release,
On earth no more the rising sun,
Shall greet thy face,—thy course is run,
The bells at midnight, toll thy knell,
Farewell ! Old Year,—a glad Farewell !

THE NEW YEAR.

The blithe New Year with aspect mild,
Appears on earth, as a little child,¹
With shining curls of auburn hair,
Clustering round his forehead fair;
Upon the world, to him so new,
He looks with eyes of softest blue;
No knowledge of the dreary past,
Hath o'er his face a shadow cast;
Little he knows of human schemes,
Joys, cares, or bold Ambition's dreams!
His fiery steeds he guides with care,
One, for each cycle of the year;
Surrounded by a radiant light,
Chasing the shadows of the night;
Bright as the rising God of Day,
And careless as a child at play;
Smiling he enters, frank and free,
The future clothed in mystery.

The smiling New Year now is King,
To him, fresh garlands earth will bring,
For him, each hour will record keep,
Of those who smile, and those who weep;
With skillful hand he draws the rein,
His whip, as yet, inflicts no pain.

We rise at midnight's witching hour,
And ring the bells in spire and tower,
Trim fire and lamp with watchful care,
In honor of this glad "New Year,"
Tossing the wine-cup in his praise,
Wishing each other "happier days."

Time,—stood between the Old and New,
As from each gate the bolts he drew,
The globe—his footstool,—firm he stands,
His hour-glass fallen from his hands;
His scythe and wings look wondrous fair,
As one departs,—one enters,—here!
The Past—his trophies, bears away,
War, conflagrations, dire dismay,—
The Present,--smiling, hopeful, blest,—
We join our voices with the rest
Who chant a pæan, loud and clear,
To hail,—"The happy, bright New Year."